# MILDRED KEITH

# The Original Mildred Classics

# MILDRED KEITH

*Book One of*
*The Original Mildred Classics*

## MARTHA FINLEY

CUMBERLAND HOUSE
NASHVILLE, TENNESSEE

Mildred Keith
by Martha Finley

Any unique characteristics of this edition:
Copyright © 2001 by Cumberland House Publishing, Inc.

Published by Cumberland House Publishing, Inc.,
431 Harding Industrial Drive, Nashville, Tennessee 37211.

Cover design by Bruce Gore, Gore Studios, Inc.
Photography by Dean Dixon Photography
Hair and Makeup by Calene Rader
Text design by Julie Pitkin

Printed in the United States of America
1 2 3 4 5 6 7 8 — 05 04 03 02 01

# MILDRED KEITH

# PREFACE

*She is pretty to walk with,*
*And witty to talk with,*
*And pleasant, too, to think on.*

— BRENNORALT

THE KEITH FAMILY were relatives of Horace Dinsmore, and as my readers will observe, the date of this story is some seven years earlier than that of the first *Elsie* book.

The journey and that most *sickly* season, which I have attempted to describe, were events in my own early childhood. The latter still dwells in my memory as a dreadful dream.

Our family—a large one—were all down with the fever except my aged grandmother and a little sister of six or seven, and "help could not be had for love or money."

My father, who was a physician, kept up and made his rounds among his town and country patients for days after the fever had attacked him, but he was at length compelled to take to his bed, and I well remember lying there beside him while the neighbors flocked into the room to consult him about their sick ones at home.

That region of country is now, I believe, as healthy as almost any other part of our favored land. Such a season, it was said, had never been known before, and there has been none like it since.

—M.F

# CHAPTER FIRST

*Weep not that the world changes —did it keep*
*A stable, changeless course, 'twere cause to weep.*

— BRYANT

A SPRING MORNING in 183– ; winter's icy breath exchanged for gentle breezes; a faint tinge of yellow green on the woods that had been until now so brown and bare; violets and anemones showing their pretty, modest faces by the roadside; hill and valley clothed with verdure; rivulets dancing and singing; the river rolling onward in majestic gladness; Apple, peach, and cherry trees in bloom; birds building their nests; men and women busy here and there in field or garden; and over all "the uncertain glory of an April day."

The sun now shining out warm and bright from a cloudless sky, now veiling his face while a sudden shower of rain sends the busy workers hurrying to the nearest shelter.

The air is full of pleasant rural sounds —the chirp of insects, the twittering of birds, the crowing of cocks —now near at hand, now far away, mellowed by the distance. In the streets of the pretty village of Lansdale, down yonder in the valley, there is the cheerful hum of busy life —of buying and selling, of tearing down and building up, neighbors chatting on doorsteps or over the garden fence, boys whistling and shouting to their mates, children working at their tasks, and mothers crooning to their babes.

Out of the side door of a substantial brick house standing far back from the street in the midst of a garden where the grass was of a velvety green spangled with violets, and snowballs and lilacs are bursting into bloom, steps a slight, girlish figure.

The face, half-hidden under a broad brimmed garden hat, is not regularly beautiful, but there is a great deal of character in it. The mouth is both firm and sweet; the lips are full and red; the eyes are large, dark, and lustrous; and the complexion is rich with the hues of health.

She sends a quick glance from side to side, clasps her hands together with a gesture as of sudden pain, paces rapidly to and fro for a moment, seemingly striving after self-control, the turning into a path that leads across the garden to the hedge that separated it from another, hastens down it, opens the gate, and passing through it, looks about as if in search of someone.

But there is no one there, and the girl trips gracefully onward to the house, a pretty cottage with vine-covered porches.

The parlor windows were open and within sat a little lady of middle age, quaintly attired in a chintz gown very short and scant and made after a pattern peculiarly her own. She was busy with brush and duster.

Catching sight of the young girl as she stepped upon the porch, she called to her in a remarkably sweet-toned voice.

"In here, dearie! Just step through the window. I'm glad to see you." The windows opened to the floor, so it was an easy matter to obey, and the girl did so, then stood silent, her lips quivering, her eyes full.

"My child, what is it?" cried the older lady, dropping her duster to take the girl's hand and draw her to a seat upon the sofa. "Is—is any one ill?"

"No, no, not that, Aunt Wealthy!" The girl valiantly swallowed down her tears and spoke with a determined effort to be calm. "But something has happened, and mother delegated me to bring you the news.

"You know father has been talking for some time of leaving Lansdale, and this morning at breakfast, he told us—us children, I mean; he and mother had talked it over last night, and I don't believe she slept much for thinking of it—that he had fully made up his mind to move out to Indiana. And we're to go just as soon as we can get ready.

"There, now you know it all!" she said, finishing with a burst of tears in spite of herself.

For a moment, her listener was dumb with surprise, but it was not in Wealthy Stanhope's nature to witness distress without an effort to comfort and relieve.

To lose the society of this family who were her nearest and dearest relatives would be a great grief to her. The mother, Marcia Keith, the orphan child

11

of a sister, who had been committed to her care in early infancy and raised by her to a lovely and useful womanhood, was as a daughter to her, and her boys and girls were as grandchildren, to be loved and petted and rejoiced over after the custom of fond grandparents. What a lonely old age for her it would be without them!

That was her first thought; the next was how to assuage the sorrow of the weeping girl at her side.

"There, there, Mildred, dear," she said, softly stroking and patting the hand she held. "Perhaps you will find it not so bad after all. There must be a bright side to the picture that we shall discover if we look for it determinately. There will be new scenes, perhaps even some adventures on the journey."

"Yes, auntie, very likely. I've often wished I could have some adventures!" Mildred answered, dashing away her tears with a rather hysterical little laugh.

"You're not going to school today?"

"No, auntie, no more school for me. That's the hard part of it, for I do so want a good education."

"Well, dear, you shall have books, and your father and mother—both educated people—will help you, and who knows but that you may, in the end, outpace your mates here. The knowledge we gain by our own efforts, out of school, is often the most serviceable."

The girl's face brightened.

"If I don't turn out to be something worthwhile, it shall not be for want of trying," she said, her cheeks flushing and her eyes sparkling.

Then, starting up, she said, "I must hurry home, for mother and I are going to work with might and main at the spring sewing and then at the tearing up and packing. Aunt Wealthy, I'm glad I'm old enough to be a help; there are so many younger ones, you know."

"Yes, Milly, and you are a great help and comfort to your mother, I am certain."

"If—if I could only learn her patience, but the children can be dreadfully trying with their untidy ways, their mischief and noise. They nearly distract me at times, and before I know it, I've given somebody a shake or a slap, or if not that, a very uncomplimentary piece of my mind," she added half laughing, half sighing.

Then with a hasty good-bye, she tripped away, her aunt calling after her, "Tell your mother I'll be in after a while."

Miss Stanhope sat where the girl had left her, the usually busy hands folded in her lap and her gaze fixed meditatively on the carpet. Presently she lifted her head with a deep-drawn sigh, and her eye passed slowly about the room, resting lovingly now upon this familiar object, now upon that.

"I don't think they would sell for much," she said musingly. "The carpet has been in wear for thirty odd years, and the colors have faded a good deal. The chairs and tables are older still, and so are the pictures on the walls. That sampler my grandmother worked when she was a young girl—which was many years ago—and these chair cushions, too—"

she said, rising and going from one to another and giving to each in turn a little loving shake and pat. "She embroidered them and filled them with her own feathers, and so I value them more than their weight in gold. Marcia, I think, values them also, but to a stranger, I suppose they would all seem old, dingy, and worthless, though to me they are real treasures. I've a sincere affection for them.

"But what is that compared to my love for Marcia and her children! What indeed!"

She hastily picked up duster and brush, gave a finishing touch here and there, drew down the blinds, and left the room.

A few moments later, she might have been seen in bonnet and shawl and armed with a large cotton umbrella, issuing from her front gate and walking briskly toward the business part of the town.

It was nearly two hours before she returned, with a step a trifle less brisk and arms filled with brown paper parcels.

She passed her own gate and stopped at Mr. Keith's.

Mildred ran to open it.

"Why, auntie, how you are loaded! Give me your bundles."

"Yes, child, carry them in to your mother. I've been to every store in town—such beautiful remnants! Couldn't help buying! They will make up pretty for the children. Afraid there's none big enough for you, dear, and I am all out of breath with walking."

"Yes, it's too bad. Don't say anything more till you're rested," said the girl, leading the way into the pleasant family room, hastily laying the packages on the table and drawing forward a large, cushioned rocking chair.

"There, sit down in this chair, auntie, and let me take your things."

"Aunt Wealthy! Come at last! We have both been wondering what kept you," said a handsome, matronly, but still youthful-looking lady with a babe in her arms, coming in at that moment. "And you've been out shopping? I hope you were not caught in any of the showers?"

"No, I managed to dodge them, sandwiching my walks in between. So, I hear you're going to leave Lansdale, Marcia?"

"Yes, auntie, and you. That's the worst of it."

The cheery voice faltered over the last words, and the bright eyes grew dim.

"Not so fast, Marcia, my dear. Who says that I'm to be left behind?"

"Aunt Wealthy! Do you mean it? Is it possible you could think of such a sacrifice?" cried Mrs. Keith, starting up and nearly dropping her babe in her intense, joyful surprise.

"As what?" queried the aunt between a smile and a tear. "Marcia, I can't give up my home, as you well know, but I have found a tenant for it—the minister and his wife, who are perfectly delighted to get it. It's their only chance for going to housekeeping, and they'll be sure to take good care of my furniture and other belongings. They rented it just as it stands for a year, and I'm going with you to Hoosier land.

"It'll be quite an importation of Buckeyes, won't it? All coming in one lot."

The good, affectionate old soul finished with a laugh, jumped up from her chair, and stretching out her arms to three little ones who had come running in while she was speaking, caught them to her bosom, kissed and cried over them, asking, "Are you glad, Cyril? Are you glad, Don? And Fan, too? Are you glad that auntie is going with you?"

There was a chorus of shouts of delight. There were huggings and kissings and the asking and answering of questions. And then things quieted down a little, and the children went back to their play, Cyril remarking, as he shut the door, "Now, I shan't cry when we go, 'cause all my friends and colations is goin' along."

"Now, to business," said Aunt Wealthy, attacking the parcels. "I'm going to help you, Marcia, in getting your tribe ready for their exodus out of this land of plenty into that western wilderness. Here are two or three dress patterns apiece for the little girls. These ones are for them to travel in, and I think they had better be made long-necked and high-sleeved. Don't you?"

Mrs. Keith looked up at her aunt with a slightly puzzled expression. Then, a light broke over her face, for she was used to her aunt's transpositions. "I don't know," she answered dubiously. "Wouldn't it make them look a little old-womanish? Low necks and short sleeves are prettier for children, I think, and they're used to it. Summer's coming on, too, and we must expect warm weather."

"What route shall you take?"

"Up the Ohio and Erie Canal and around Michigan by the lakes."

"It will be cool on the water."

"Yes, that's true. I'll take your advice."

"That's right. They'll be less likely to catch cold from any little exposure, and their necks and arms will be protected from the sun. Now, if you'll tear off a skirt, I'll get to work. I brought my thimble and scissors along."

Those were not the days of sewing machines, and though garments were made in a much simpler style than now, the sewing for such a family as the Keiths was no small task.

It would take some weeks of very diligent work by three or four pairs of hands to accomplish what the mother deemed necessary in the way of preparing their wardrobe for the contemplated journey.

Under the instruction of her mother and aunt, Mildred had already become as accomplished a needlewoman as either of them. A seamstress had been engaged to assist but could not be had for a few days, so plans and prospects could be talked over freely as the three sat and worked together, with baby Annis asleep in her cradle or playing contentedly on the carpet at her mother's feet.

# CHAPTER SECOND

*The mother in her office, holds the key of the soul
And she it is who stamps the coin of character,
And makes the being who would be a savage,
But for her gentle cares, a Christian man.*

—OLD PLAY

THE STRIKING OF the town clock, the ringing of bells, the blowing of whistles, and "the schoolboy's glad shout" announced the noontide hour.

A sound of coming footsteps, of happy young voices, an opening of doors letting in fresh breezes from without, and with them two bright, blooming, merry little girls and a lad between them and Mildred in age, in whose great black eyes lurked a world of fun and mischief.

"Softly, softly, children," the mother said, looking up with a smile as they came dancing and prancing in. "Rupert, are you not old enough to begin to act in a rather more gentlemanly way?"

"Yes, mother, I beg your pardon. Yours, too, Aunt Wealthy. I didn't know till this moment that you were here."

"Mother, he's always teasing," complained the younger of the girls. "He says we'll have to live in wigwams like the Indians and perhaps grow to be as brown as they are."

"But they're not brown, Ada," exclaimed the other. "My g'ography book calls 'em 'red men.'"

"If you're careful to wear your sunbonnets when you go out, you won't grow to be either," said Mildred.

Mrs. Keith said, with a look of mild reproof, "Rupert, my son, was it quite truthful to tell your sisters such things?"

"I was only making fun," he answered, trying to turn it off with a laugh but blushing as he spoke.

"Innocent fun I never object to, but sport is too dearly bought at the sacrifice of truth. "My boy," she added with energy, "one should go to the stake rather than tell a falsehood, though it were no more than to say that two and two do not make four."

"Mother, I believe I would!" he said, gazing with loving admiration into her earnest face. "I've never known you to swerve a hair's breadth from the truth in any way," he said. And coming close to her side and speaking almost in a whisper, he added, "I mean to try to be worthy of you in the future."

She looked at him with glistening eyes, and dropping her work, she took his hands in hers for a moment.

The others were not listening. Zillah and Ada had caught sight of the new dresses and were admiring them and asking eager questions of their aunt and sister.

"My boy," Mrs. Keith said in moved tones, "I would rather be the mother of a poor, hard-working man of whom it could be said that he had always been perfectly honest and true than of one who had amassed his millions and attained the highest worldly honors by fraud or questionable deeds or words. Remember that all your life, son."

"Mother, I will. I have my father's example to help me, as well as yours," the lad replied with a proud glance at the noble, kindly, intellectual face of a gentleman who came in at that instant with Fan in his arms and the two little boys gamboling about him.

"Ah, Aunt Wealthy. Good morning!" he said in a cheery tone, sitting down beside her, putting Fan on one knee, and lifting the babe, who was laughing and crowing with delight at the sight of him, to the other. "I suppose you have heard the news?"

"That you are going to Indiana, Stuart? Yes. You are not contented to let well enough alone?"

"Can't consider it well enough to be barely making the two ends meet while a growing family must be constantly increasing my expenses."

"How is this removal to help you? It will cost a good deal."

"'Nothing ventured, nothing gained.' I'm going to a new country where land is cheap. I shall invest something in that and hope to see it increase largely in value as the town grows.

"Also, lawyers are not so plentiful there, and more will be needed as people move in. I hope that by being on the spot in good season, I can secure an extensive practice.

"It will cost the sundering of some very tender ties," he continued, his face growing grave almost to sadness, "but we are willing to bear that for our children's sakes. Is it not so, wife?" He turned to her with a smile that spoke volumes of love and confidence.

"Yes, indeed, Stuart," she answered with cheerful heartiness. "I shouldn't have hesitated for a moment if I had been quite sure it would be the best thing for them. But, as you know, I'm afraid we cannot give them as good an education there as we might here. However, we have now decided to go, and I can only hope for the best.

"And do you know," she went on with a smile directed to the corner where Miss Stanhope sat, "that since you left us this morning something has happened that takes away more than half the pain of the thought of leaving Lansdale?"

"No. What may that be?"

"Oh, I know!" shouted Cyril, turning a somersault on the carpet. "Aunt Wealthy's goin' along! Aunt Wealthy's goin' along!"

And then such raptures of delight were indulged in by those who had not heard the news before!

These were interrupted by a summons to the dinner table, but when the blessing had been asked and the plates filled, the talk went on again, though in a somewhat more subdued fashion.

"Is there absolutely no danger from the Indians, Stuart?" asked Miss Stanhope.

"None whatever. Most of the tribes have moved to

the far west—all but one, I think, and they will probably go soon."

"What tribe is it? The Wottapottamies?"

"Pottawottamies. Yes."

"Father, will we have to live in wigwams and dress in animal skins?" asked Ada, anxiously.

"No. We'll have a house, even if it is only a log cabin, and we'll carry plenty of clothes along."

"P'raps dey might det losted on the way," suggested Fan.

"Well, kitten, I think we'll find some stores out there, and if everything else fails, we can always fall back on deerskins."

Lansdale was but a small town. Everybody in it knew the Keiths or knew of them, and by the next day after their move had been decided upon, everybody knew that.

Many regrets were expressed, and there were some offers of assistance with their preparations, but these were declined with thanks. "With Aunt Wealthy's good help and that of the seamstress already engaged," Mrs. Keith said, "she and Mildred would be able to do all that was necessary."

They were very busy cutting, fitting, and sewing, day after day, from morning to night, with occasional interruptions from the little ones who were too young to go to school but old enough to roam over house and grounds. Being adventurous spirits, full of life and energy, the little ones were constantly getting into mischief, thus furnishing, gratis, a change of work to mother and eldest sister, who, in spite of a hearty affection for the young rogues, was often sorely tried by their pranks.

"Have you any cord, Mrs. Keith?" asked the young seamstress one morning.

"Yes," she replied, turning to her workbasket. "Why, what has become of it? I had two or three pieces here. And that paper of needles has also disappeared! Mildred did you—?"

"The children were here half an hour ago, mother. I remember seeing Donald peeping into your basket."

"Run out and see what they have done with them."

Going into the hall, Mildred stood a moment listening for some sound to tell her where the children were. Little voices were prattling in the garden near at hand. Stepping to the door, she saw the two boys seated on the grass, busy with a kite Rupert had made for them.

"What are you doing?" she asked, going nearer.

"Makin' a longer tail."

"Where did you get that piece of cord?"

No answer; only guilty looks on two chubby faces.

"Oh, I know! It's some cord you took from mother's workbasket. And now it's wanted, but you've spoiled it entirely. Boys, why did you cut and knot it so?"

"Why," said Cyril, "you see, Don was my crazy man, and I had to tie him, then I had to cut the string to get it off, 'cause I couldn't untie the knots."

"Oh, you mischievous fellows. Next time, don't take things without asking. Did you take a paper of needles, too?"

"No, we didn't. Maybe Fan did."

Mildred went in search of Fan and found her digging and planting in her little garden, the empty needle paper lying nearby.

"Fan," said Mildred, picking it up, "what have you done with the needles that were in this paper?"

"Sowed 'em in dis bed. When dey drows up, we'll have lots an' lots for mother an' you."

"You silly, provoking little kitten. Needles don't grow. Show me where you put them."

"Tan't. Dey's all 'round in de gwound."

Mildred took up a bit of a stick and poked in the fresh earth for a minute or two, then, remarking to herself that it was as fruitless as hunting in a haystack, went into the house with the report of the hapless fate of the missing articles.

The boys were there before her, penitently exhibiting the ruined cord and promising to do so no more.

"We didn't fink, mother," pleaded Don, looking up into her face with such a droll mixture of fun and entreaty in his roguish blue eyes that she could not refrain from giving him a kiss and a smile as she answered.

"Ah, my boys must learn to think and not take mother's things without leave. Now, run away to your play and try to be good children."

"Mother, I do think you're a little too easy with them," Mildred said in a slightly vexed tone.

"Perhaps. But if I make a mistake, is it not far better to do so on the side of mercy than of severity?"

"I suppose so. I shouldn't like to see them whipped."

Then, laughingly, she told the story of Fan's doings, and as needles and cord must be replaced, put on her bonnet and sallied forth upon the errand.

Mildred was one of the prettiest, most accomplished, graceful, and fascinating young ladies around and, belonging to one of the prominent families, was a great deal admired and never lacked for attention at a party, picnic, or any sort of gathering of the young people of the town.

As she left the store where she had made her purchases, Spencer Hall crossed the street and joined her.

He was the only son of the wealthiest man in the town and, because of his great expectations, was looked upon by most of the young girls and their mamas as a desirable match.

Mildred, however, was of a different opinion, knowing him to be idle, purse-proud, vain, and also conceited.

She therefore returned his greeting rather coldly, heartily wishing that he had not happened to see her or that something would occur to rid her at once of his undesirable company.

Greatly amazed would the exquisite young man have been could he have read her thoughts, for he had no doubt that she felt highly gratified and honored by his notice. Was he not arrayed in broadcloth suit, silk hat, and immaculate kid gloves, while she wore calico, cotton gloves, and the simplest of straw bonnets? And could not his father buy hers out ten times over?

His manner was gracious and patronizing as he remarked, sauntering along by her side, "Why, Miss Mildred, can it be true that you are going to leave us? I don't see what Lansdale will do without you."

"It is quite true that we are going, Mr. Hall," she answered with a slight curl of the lip. "And I suppose my father and mother will be missed, but I cannot think that my loss will in any way affect the prosperity of the town or the happiness of its people."

"Some people's it certainly will," he said with increased graciousness, exerting himself slightly to keep pace with her as she quickened her steps to a very rapid walk. "We don't want to lose you. Might it not be possible to persuade you to remain among us?"

"Certainly not, unless my parents should change their plans and decide to stay, of which there is not the least probability."

"Do you know that you are walking very fast, Miss Mildred?" he said, laughing. "Do let us slacken our pace a little, for who knows when we may have the pleasure of walking together again."

"You must excuse me. I am in great haste, but there is not the least necessity for your exerting yourself to keep pace with me. It is broad daylight, and I know the way."

"Now don't be sarcastic, my dear young lady. I'd be willing at any time to make a far greater exertion for the pleasure of your society, but if we move so rapidly, it will shorten our interview considerably."

"I have already explained that I am in haste. There is much to be done in the few weeks before we leave," the girl answered coldly, pressing on with accelerated speed.

"Haven't time even for a word with an old friend, eh? Then good morning, Miss Keith," and turning about in disgust, he sauntered along in another direction while she sped along her way as before.

"Is it possible? What does the girl mean?" he exclaimed the next minute, as on turning his head to look after her, he perceived that Mildred had actually stopped upon the sidewalk—stopped to speak to a mutual acquaintance, a lad a year or two younger than himself, who was working his own way in the world, getting an education by own effort, and helping a widowed, invalid mother.

For Frank Osborne, Mildred had the highest respect, though she looked upon him as a mere boy and was wholly unconscious that to him she was the embodiment of every virtue and grace, that her words, looks, and smiles were treasured up in his heart of hearts. Nor did she dream how unhesitatingly he would have laid down his life to save hers had it been in danger. It was only a boy's passion, but it was deep and strong.

The news of the intended removal of the Keiths to what, in those days, seemed a far-distant region, had been a great shock to him. But with the hopefulness of youth, he consoled himself with the resolve to follow and seek her out—when in the course of years he should earn fame and fortune—though she should be carried to the ends of the earth.

His eye brightened and his cheek flushed as, on turning a corner, he came suddenly upon her in her rapid walk. She stopped and held out her hand in friendly greeting.

He took it almost reverently.

"How d'ye do, Frank? And how is your mother today?" she was saying, her bright eyes looking straight into his.

"Better, thank you, Miss Mildred. And you are well? Oh, can it be true that you are all going so far away?" he asked with a wistful, longing look.

"Yes, to the land of the Hoosiers, wild Indians, and wolves," she said merrily. "Don't you envy me?"

"I envy those that go with you," he answered, sighing. "You won't forget old friends, Miss Mildred?"

"No. No, indeed, Frank," she said heartily. "But good-bye. I must hurry home," and with a nod and a smile she tripped away, to the satisfaction of Hall, who had jealously watched the whole interview.

He was glad it had been no longer, though he could not avoid the unpleasant consciousness that more time and favor had been shown to "that pauper" than to himself, the prospective heir to a very comfortable fortune.

# CHAPTER THIRD

*Lessons so dear, so fraught with holy truth
As those her mother's faith shed on her youth.*

"NOW," SAID MILDRED, taking up her sewing again, "I must work fast to make up for lost time, for I've set my heart on finishing this dress of Ada's today."

The words had scarcely left her lips when there came a loud crash and scream from the hall, followed by a sound of tumbling and rolling.

Up sprang mother, aunt, and sister, scattering scissors, thimbles, and work, and they rushed toward the scene of the commotion.

They found the stairs and Fan, who sat weeping halfway up, drenched with water, while at the foot were scattered fragments of a large pitcher. Cyril lay among them half-stunned and with blood streaming from a cut on his head. Don gazed down upon him from the landing, adding his bit to the confusion by screaming, "Oh! Oh! Oh! He's deaded! He's deaded!"

"No, he ain't," said Cyril, slowly getting to his feet. "Mother, I didn't mean to. Please don't let Milly scold us young ones. Oh, stop this quick!" he said, putting his hand to his head.

"Yes, sonny, as soon as possible," said Mrs. Keith, taking his head in her hands and holding the lips of the wound together. "A basin of cold water, Milly, quick! And aunt, there is sticking plaster in the worktable drawer. Hush, Don. Don't cry anymore, Fan. Cyril isn't much hurt, and mother will soon make it right."

Her orders were promptly obeyed, the wound skillfully dressed, Fan's wet clothes changed, and then inquiry was made as to how it had all happened.

"Why—why," said Cyril, "you see, Fan wanted to wash her hands 'cause she'd been diggin' in her garden, and dey was all dirty. Dere wasn't any water in the pitcher, and so we brung it down and got it full. I was carryin' it up, and my foot tripped. I fell down with it and knocked Fan over 'cause she was behind me. I couldn't help it. Could I, Don?"

"No, you touldna help it," assented Don. "And Fan touldn't, too."

"And he's dot a bad hurt on his head," put in Fan pityingly.

"Yes, he's punished enough, I think," said the mother, caressing him. "His intentions seem to have been good, but next time you want water, dears, come and tell mother or sister Milly."

"There, the morning's gone," said Mildred, as bells and whistles began their usual announcement. "A full hour of it wasted, too, by the pranks of these children. I hope they've finished up the business for today!"

Vain hope! Inactivity was impossible to those

restless spirits, and their surplus energy must be worked off in some way.

They had not been heard from for two hours, and Mrs. Keith had just remarked that she feared it must be some mischief that was keeping them so quiet when shrieks and wails from three infantile voices, coming from the second story, appealed strongly to the compassion of their relatives in the sitting room.

The call for help was responded to as promptly as on the previous occasion. Mother, aunt, and sister flew to the rescue, and on entering the room whence the sounds proceeded, they found Fan locked in the wardrobe and the two boys seated in the lower drawer of the bureau which their weight had caused to tip so far forward that they could not get out without assistance. A chair standing so near as to prevent the bureau from falling entirely to the floor had saved them from a serious accident, but there they were, bent nearly double, legs dangling, vociferous screams issuing from their throats.

It was the work of a moment for the laughing mother and aunt to lift up the bureau and release the two rogues, while Mildred sprang to the wardrobe, unlocked it, and took the sobbing Fan in her arms.

"You poor dear, who fastened you in there?"

"Cyril did. He said I stealed and must go to jail. And—and I was 'f'aid it would des tumble over. It shaked so when I tried to det out."

"The naughty boy!" cried Mildred, flashing an indignant glance at him as he and Don crept from the drawer, straightened themselves, and stood looking very much abashed and ill at ease.

"Mother, I do think Cyril ought to be punished."

"I didn't hurt her," he muttered, hanging his head. "And I was goin' to let her out 'fore long. And we didn't mean to tumble the bureau over. Did we, Don?"

"No, it dus went yight over its ownse'f," chimed in the little brother. "Please, mamma, we's doein' to be dood boys now."

"You might have been very much hurt if the chair had not been where it was," she said, composing her features and speaking with becoming gravity. "I am thankful for your escape, and you must never do such things again. Especially never lock each other into a wardrobe or closet," she added sitting down, drawing Fan to her side and caressing her tenderly, while Miss Stanhope and Mildred restored the contents of the bureau drawer which the boys had unceremoniously tossed upon the carpet.

"Why, mother?" queried the self-constituted jailer.

"Because it is very dangerous. Your little sister might have been frightened into a fit or have died for want of air to breathe."

Cyril's eyes dilated, then filled with tears as he seemed to see the little sister he loved so dearly lying before him white and cold and dead.

"I won't ever, ever, ever do it again, mamma," he said quite tremulously.

"No, you must be Fan's big, brave brother that she can trust to take care of her and shield her from harm. I don't believe my Cyril would be such a mean coward as to hurt a little girl or anything smaller or weaker than himself, except for that naughty, 'didn't think!'"

"But I didn't hurt her, mother."

"Yes, my son, you hurt her feelings very much."

He considered a moment. "Yes, I s'pose that's so," he said slowly. "Fan, I'll tell you, I'm real sorry, and you may be jailer now and lock me up in that dark wardrobe."

"No, no! There must be no more such doings," quickly interposed mamma.

"Dess I wouldn't do such sing!" said Fan, wiping away her tears with her chubby little hand.

"What a room!" said Mildred, shutting the last bureau drawer and turning to look about her. "Every chair out of place and turned on its side, the bed tumbled, and bits of paper scattered all over the carpet."

"Pick them up, children, and try to keep out of mischief for the rest of the day. I must go back to my sewing," Mrs. Keith said, following her aunt, who had already left the room.

Mildred stayed behind to assist in setting the room to rights. "You naughty children! Really, I could almost enjoy spanking you all around," she exclaimed directly, as she came upon the fragments of a delicate china vase belonging to herself and a valued letter from a friend torn into bits.

"Milly," said Cyril solemnly, "s'pose we should get deaded some day. Wouldn't you be sorry?"

"Suppose I should get deaded," she retorted. "Wouldn't you be sorry for spoiling my pretty things?"

She was ashamed of her outburst nevertheless, and the child's words haunted her all that afternoon.

It was evening. Two candles burned on the sitting room table, and beside it sat Mildred and her mother still busily plying their needles.

The rest of the family were in bed, and Miss Stanhope and the seamstress had gone to their own homes hours ago.

"My child, put up your work for tonight," said Mrs. Keith. "You are looking weary and depressed, and no wonder, for you have had a hard day."

"A busy day, mother, but not so hard as yours, because I have had a walk in the fresh air while you have been stitch-stitching from early morning till now. And if you don't forbid it, I shall sit up and work as long as you do. I consider it one of the eldest daughter's privileges to share her mother's burdens."

"My dear girl! You are a comfort to me! I thank God for you every day," the mother said, looking at her with dewy eyes and a beautiful smile. "But because you are young and growing, you need more rest and sleep than I do. So go, daughter, and never mind leaving me."

"Mayn't I stay a little longer?" pleaded the girl. "I want one of our nice confidential talks. Oh, mother, I am so disgusted with myself! I was very angry with Cyril and Don today when I found they'd broken that vase that I valued so — because you gave it to me as a birthday present and it was so pretty, too—and tore up that sweet letter dear Miss Grey wrote me just before she died."

"Indeed! I didn't know they had done such damage, and I am very sorry for your loss, dear!"

"Yes, mother, I knew you would be. My loss of temper, though, was worse than all. I do wish I knew how you contrive always to be so patient."

"I'm afraid it's very often all on the outside," the mother answered with a slight smile. "But I find it a great help in bearing patiently with the little everday worries, to think of them as sent, or permitted, by my best Friend—the One who never makes a mistake—for my growth in grace. For you know we grow strong by resistance."

"Well, mother, I am constantly resolving that I will not give way to my temper, and yet I keep doing so. I grow so discouraged and so disgusted with myself. What shall I do?"

"My child, watch and pray. Our sufficiency is of God. He is our strength. And do not look at yourself; try to forget self altogether in 'looking unto Jesus.' Get your mind and heart full of His lovely image— so full that there will be no room in it for aught else—and thus shall you grow into His likeness."

Mildred's eyes shone as she looked up into her mother's earnest face.

"I am sure that must be the way," she said, low and with feeling, "and I will try it, for I do long to be like Him, mother. He is, indeed to me, 'the chiefest among ten thousand and the one altogether lovely!'"

"Oh, how good He is to me!" exclaimed the mother, glad tears shining in her eyes. "That you might learn thus to know and love Him has been the burden of my prayer for you—for each of my dear children—since they first saw the light."

They worked on in silence for some minutes, then Mildred, seeing a smile playing about her mother's lips, asked what was the thought that provoked it.

"A reminiscence of some of your infantile pranks," her mother answered, laughing. "You should be forbearing with your little brothers and sisters, for you were fully as mischievous as they are.

"Before you could walk, I caught you one day seated in the middle of the table set for tea with your hand in the sugar bowl, your mouth full, and your face besmeared.

"You were a great climber, and it was difficult to keep anything out of your way. And as soon as Rupert could creep, he followed you into danger and mischief, pulling things about, breaking, tearing, cutting, climbing fences and trees, and even getting out of the windows onto roofs.

"Besides, you two had a perfect mania for tasting everything that could possibly be eaten or drunk— soap, candles, camphor, lye, medicines, whatever you could lay your hands on—till I was in constant fear for your lives."

"You poor, dear mother. What a time you must have had with us!" exclaimed the girl. "We can never hope to repay you for your patient love and care."

"My child, I have always felt that my darlings paid for their trouble as they went along. Their love has always been so sweet to me," Mrs. Keith answered cheerily. "And I cannot tell you how much I enjoy the sweet society and confidence of my eldest daughter—the knowledge that she has no secrets from me."

"I have not, indeed," Mildred said, heartily. "And why should I, knowing as I do that my mother is my best and wisest, as well as dearest, earthly friend?"

Then, recalling the events of the morning, she gave a laughing account of her encounter in town with Spencer Hall.

"If I could even contemplate the possibility of leaving you behind, it would certainly not be in his care," her mother said, joining in her merriment. "I am glad you have sense enough not to fancy him."

"Truly, I do not in the least, though many of the girls consider him a great catch because of his father's wealth," said Mildred. "But really, I don't believe he meant anything, and I felt like showing him that I understood that very well and resented his trifling, and wouldn't have been much better pleased if he had been in earnest."

# CHAPTER FOURTH

*And, like some low and mournful spell,*
*To whisper but one word—farewell.*

— PARK BENJAMIN

ONE SWEET JUNE morning, a very expectant group gathered in the cool shade of the vine-wreathed porch of Miss Stanhope's pretty cottage. It consisted of that good lady herself and Mr. and Mrs. Keith and their eight children, who were all attired in neat traveling costumes and awaiting the coming of the stagecoach, which was to carry them the first step of their journey, to the nearest town situated on the Ohio and Erie Canal.

Mr. and Mrs. Park, the new occupants of the cottage, were there, too, and a few old neighbors and friends who had run in for a last good-bye.

Mrs. Keith and Mildred turned every now and then with a very tearful lingering look upon their deserted home and this other which was equally familiar and almost equally dear. Miss Stanhope seemed to have some ado to control her feelings of sadness and anxiety for the future, but Mr. Keith was in fine spirits, in which the children evidently shared very largely.

Eager to be off, they moved restlessly about, asking again and again, "When will the stage come?" and kept sending out reconnoitering parties to see if there were any signs of its approach.

At length, they espied it and announced the fact with joyful exclamations as its four prancing steeds came sweeping around the corner and, swaying and rolling, it dashed up to the gate.

The driver drew rein, and the guard sprang from his lofty perch, threw open the door, and let down the steps.

There were hurried embraces and farewells, and a hasty stowing away of bags, bundles, and passengers large and small on the inside, and more bulky baggage in the boot of the coach. The steps were replaced, the door slammed to, and amid the waving of handkerchiefs and a chorus of good-byes and good wishes, the "toot-toot!" of the guard's horn, and the crack of the coachman's whip, they swept away down the street, looking, in all probability, their last upon many a well-known object and many a friendly face, nodding and smiling to them from door or window.

Frank Osborne, at work in his mother's garden, dropped his hoe to lift his hat and bow as the stage passed and to gaze after it with a longing and lingering look.

Spencer Hall, standing, cigar in mouth, on the steps of his father's mansion, did likewise.

But Mildred had turned her head away, purposely, and did not see him.

Never before had Lansdale put on so inviting an appearance, nor had the surrounding country looked so lovely as today, while they rolled onward through the valley and over the hills now clothed in all the rich verdure of early summer and basking in the brilliant sunlight occasionally mellowed and subdued by the flitting shadow of some soft, white, fleecy-like cloud floating in the deep azure of the sky.

A few hours' drive took the travelers to the town where they were to exchange the stage for the canal boat, the packet *Pauline*. She lay at the wharf, and having dined comfortably at a hotel nearby, they went on board, taking with them the luggage brought by the stage.

Their household goods had been dispatched on the same route some days before.

Here they were in quarters only less confined than those of the stage, the *Pauline*'s cabin being so narrow that when the table was set for a meal, most of the passengers had to go on deck to be out of the way.

All along the side of the cabin ran a cushioned seat that was used for dining purposes in the daytime and as a lower berth at night. Other shelf-like berths could then set up over it—all so narrow that the occupant could scarcely turn upon his couch, and the upper ones so close to the ceiling that it required some care to avoid striking one's head against it in getting in or out. Also, there was also an unpleasant dampness about the bedding.

In the cool of the evening or when the sun was clouded, the deck was the favorite place of resort.

But there a constant lookout for bridges must be kept, and to escape them, it was sometimes necessary to throw one's self flat upon the deck — not the most pleasant of alternatives.

The progress of these packets was so slow, too, that it took nearly a week to reach Cleveland from the point where Miss Stanhope and the Keiths had embarked.

But this mode of travel had its compensations. One was the almost absolute safety, another the ease with which the voyager could step ashore when the boat was in a lock and refresh himself with a brisk walk along the tow-path, boarding her again when the next lock was reached.

This was done daily by some of the Keith family, even the very young ones being sometimes allowed the treat when the weather and walking were fine and the distance was not too great.

Passengers were constantly getting off and on at the locks and the towns along the route, and often the boat was crowded. It was so the first night that our friends spent on board.

Babies cried, older children fretted, and some grown people indulged in loud complaints of scant and uncomfortable accommodations. Altogether, the cabin was a scene of confusion, and the younger Keiths felt very forlorn.

But mother, aunt, and older sister were patient, soothing, comforting, and at length succeeding in getting them all to sleep.

Then Aunt Wealthy, saying that she felt disposed to lie down and rest beside the children, persuaded Mrs. Keith and Mildred to go upon the deck for an hour to enjoy the moonlight and the pleasant evening breeze with Mr. Keith and Rupert, who had been there ever since supper.

Mr. Keith helped his wife and daughter up the short flight of steps that led from the stern to the deck and found them seats on some of their own trunks.

There were a number of other passengers sitting about or pacing to and fro, among them a burly German who sat flat on the deck at the stern end of the boat, his long legs dangling over the edge, his elbow on his knee and his bearded chin in his hand, gazing out idly over the moonlight landscape while wreaths of smoke from a pipe in his mouth curled slowly up from his lips.

The *Pauline* glided onward with easy, pleasant motion. All had grown quiet in the cabin below, and the song of the bullfrogs, the dull thud of the horses' hoofs, and the gentle rush of the water against the sides of the boat were the only sounds that broke the stillness.

"How nice it is here here!" exclaimed Mildred. "The breeze is so refreshing and the moonlight so enchanting!"

"Yes, the country is looking beautiful," said her mother, "and one can get a good view of it here, but I feel somewhat apprehensive in regard to the bridges. We must be on the watch for them and dodge them in time."

"We will," said her husband, "though we may pretty safely trust the steersman. It is his duty to be on the lookout and give timely warning."

"Well, we're facing the right direction to see them," remarked Rupert, "but that German back there is not. I s'pose he's safe enough, though, with the man at the helm to sing out as we near them."

With that, they fell into talk on other topics and thought no more of the smoker.

"Bridge!" sang out the steersman, and down went every head except that of the German, who sat and smoked on unmoved.

"Bridge!" The cry was repeated in louder and more emphatic tones.

"Yah, pridge, pridge!" responded the German, straightening up a little and nodding his head quite assentingly, but he did not look around.

"Bridge!" sang out the steersman for the third time. "Bridge, you stupid lout! Dodge or —"

But the boat was already sweeping under, and the bridge hitting the German across his shoulders, threw him with sudden violence to the platform below, whence he rolled over into the canal, uttering a half- stifled cry for help as the water closed over him.

But he rose again instantly, panting and spluttering and striking out vigorously for the boat. He presently succeeded in laying hold of the edge of the platform, and with the steersman lending him a helping hand, he clambered on board, crestfallen and dripping, while the crowd on the deck, seeing him safe, indulged in a hearty laugh at his expense.

"I loss mein bipe," he said ruefully, shrugging his shoulders and shaking the water from his clothes.

"Well, you got a free bath in exchange and may be thankful you didn't lose your life," remarked the steersman with a grin. "Next time I call out bridge, I guess you'll duck your head like the rest."

⚓ ⚓ ⚓

The rain had been falling heavily all night, but the sun now shone brightly, and the clouds were flying before a high wind that blew fresh and cool from Lake Erie as the *Pauline* glided quietly into the city of Cleveland.

"What a beautiful city!" exclaimed the young Keiths, as they stepped ashore. "Please, let us walk to the hotel, father, if it is not too far."

"Just as Aunt Wealthy and your mother say," he replied, taking the baby from his wife. "I am told it is but a short distance, Marcia. I will have our heavy baggage carried directly to the steamer which leaves this afternoon; Rupert and the older girls can take charge of the satchels and small packages."

The ladies decided in favor of the walk as affording agreeable exercise and enabling them to see the city to better advantage than if cooped up in a hack or omnibus. No one regretted their choice. They found the wide streets so clean and the breeze so refreshing and exhilarating, and enjoyed very much gazing upon the tall, elegant-looking houses and the pretty things displayed in the windows of the large, handsome stores.

After a good dinner at the hotel, Mr. Keith, his wife, and his older children went out for another stroll about the city. Miss Stanhope, who insisted that she had had exercise enough and preferred to stay where she was, took charge of the little ones.

On the return of the pedestrians, the whole party went on board the steamer which was to convey them across the lake to Detroit. It was a fine boat, the cabins large and handsome, with staterooms on each side that were furnished with berths of far more comfortable size than those of the canal packets.

The table here was better, too, both in its appointments and the quality of the food. It was set in a lower salon, reached from the upper one by a flight of broad, winding stairs.

The children were delighted with the change and wanted to be on the railings all afternoon, watching the play of the great stern wheel, admiring the rainbows in the clouds of spray it sent up, looking out over the wide expanse of water at the islands and an occasional passing boat, or racing back and forth.

Mildred and Rupert were given charge of the three little ones and found great vigilance necessary to prevent Cyril and Don from putting themselves in peril of their lives. Mildred was more than once sorely tempted to shake the younger rogues who gave her no peace, but, remembering and acting upon her mother's advice, she was able to restrain herself and treat them with uniform gentleness.

She felt rewarded when, as she was putting them to bed, her mother being busy with the babe, Don threw his arms impulsively around her neck and, kissing her again and again, said, "I loves you, Milly; you so dood to us naughty chillens."

"That she is!" assented Cyril, heartily. "An' I wish I didn't be so bad."

"Well, try again tomorrow to be ever so good," Mildred answered, tucking them in and leaving them with a goodnight kiss.

She helped her sisters with their preparations for the night, then was rewarded with a delightful evening spent with the older members of the family in the open air, looking out upon the beautiful, wide expanse of waters, now starlit and illumined by the silvery rays of the moon as she rose from the distant eastern edge of the lake and slowly ascended the azure vault of the heavens, now shining resplendently and again veiling her fair face for a moment with a thin, floating cloud.

The next morning the steamer lay at anchor in Detroit harbor, and our friends left her for a hotel on what was then the principal street of the city. Here, too, they walked out to view the land, and passing stores and public buildings, found well-shaded streets and handsome residences with pretty yards in front.

Mr. Keith gave his children their choice of passing around the lakes in a steamer or in the sloop *Queen*

*Charlotte.* They chose the latter, and the next morning the family and their luggage were transferred to her decks.

The ladies pointed out the articles they wished carried to their staterooms and followed the bearers.

There was less show here than on the steamer they had left, but comfort and convenience had not been overlooked, and though Mildred's face clouded a little, it brightened again in a moment as she noted the cheerful content in those of her mother and aunt.

They hurried on deck again where Rupert had been left in charge of the younger children, to watch the vessel getting under way.

They were lying close to a steamer on whose other side was a second sloop in quite close proximity. All seemed hurry and bustle on board the three.

"I don't see how we are to start," observed Mildred, glancing up at the sails that hung almost motionless on the masts, "for there's scarcely a breath of wind."

"Don't you see that they're lashing us and the *Milwaukee* yonder fast to the steamboat, one on each side?" said Rupert. "She's to tow both till the wind gets up."

"Oh, is that the way? She'll have hard work to do it, I should think."

"She won't growl anyway."

"No, I suppose not. Which is the captain, Ru?"

"That nice, jolly-looking chap over yonder that's giving orders in such a loud peremptory tone is

Captain Wells, master of the ship. That blue-eyed, brown-haired, rosy-cheeked stripling standing near is his son, Edward Wells. And they're both English, so don't remind them that this vessel was taken from the British in the last war."

"Of course not, unless they say something mean or exasperating about Washington or America."

"In that case, I give you leave to tweak 'em as hard as you like."

"Who was that nice man that helped us on board? I thought father or somebody called him captain."

"So he is. Captain Jones—but acting as first mate here. That lady talking to mother and Aunt Wealthy is his wife. They're both Yankees, so you can relieve your mind occasionally on the subject of the ship by a little private exultation with them.

"Do you notice the contrast between those two faces—mother's and Mrs. Jones's? Hers is so dark, and mother's so beautifully fair and rosy."

"Who could help noticing it? Rupert, I do think our mother has just the loveliest face in the world!"

"Ditto!" he said, gazing at her with a world of filial love, pride, and chivalric admiration in his handsome eyes.

"I say what's the use? You may just as well set still where you are," growled a voice near at hand.

The young people turned involuntarily at the sound, and they perceived that the speaker was a burly, red-faced, young Englishman. The one not so politely or kindly addressed, a little meek-eyed woman of the same nationality with a chalky complexion and washed out appearance, who, as they afterward learned and suspected at the time, was his wife.

"What a bear!" exclaimed Rupert in an aside to his sister, drawing her away as he spoke. "See, we're beginning to move. Let's go over to the other side where we can have a better view."

"I presume that's what she wanted to do," remarked Mildred, glancing back at the meek-eyed woman. "And why shouldn't he have let her?"

"Why, indeed, except that he's a cowardly bully."

"How do you know?"

"Because that's the only kind of man that would speak so to a decent woman."

# CHAPTER FIFTH

*Hark! to the hurried question of despair:*
*Where is my child? and echo answers "where!"*

— BYRON

"HOW DID YOU learn all you've been telling me, Ru?" asked Mildred, as they stood side by side watching with interest the *Queen Charlotte* and her consorts slowly clearing the harbor. "Oh, easily enough. Young Wells and I got to talking while you and the others were down in the cabin. I asked questions, and he answered 'em. Ah, here he comes," he added, looking around. "I'll introduce him, for he's a nice fellow, I'm sure, and it's a good thing to have a friend at court—in other words, to be in favor with the reigning powers, i.e., the captain and his nearest kin. My sister, Miss Mildred Keith, Mr. Wells."

"Happy to make your acquaintance, Miss," said the young sailor gallantly, lifting his hat and bowing low. "I hope you'll enjoy your voyage on the *Queen Charlotte*. I shall be most happy to do all I can to make the trip pleasant for you."

"Thank you kindly."

He began at once to find comfortable seats for them where they were sheltered from the sun and had a good view of the Canada and Michigan shores.

Being acquainted with the localities and their history and possessed of a ready command of language, he added much to the interest of the scene by the information he imparted—sometimes unsolicited, at others in answer to direct questions.

When they had passed through the Detroit River and so far out into Lake St. Claire that little could be seen but water and sky, he offered to show them the vessel.

They gladly accepted, enjoyed the tour, and when it was over, rejoined the rest of their party just as the cabin passengers were summoned to their supper table.

Mildred was seated between Rupert and Edward Wells. Opposite them sat Mr. and Mrs. Sims, the bullying Englishman and his meek-eyed wife, and a bachelor gentleman of pleasing countenance and manners, whom Captain Wells addressed as Mr. Carr. Next to them were Captain and Mrs. Jones. There were many more passengers of both sexes, several nationalities, and a variety of ages—from infants in arms up to hoary-headed grandparents—but with most of them, our story has little to do.

The two captains, the wife of the one, and the son of the other, were very polite and rather genial. The fare was excellent, and everyone present seemed disposed to contentment and good humor except Mr. Sims, who turned up his nose at the food, snubbed his wife, and scowled at his opposite neighbors, perchance because he read too plainly in their frank, youthful countenance their disapproval of him.

Mildred so sympathized with the long-suffering wife that, in the course of the evening, seeing her sitting by herself and looking sad and lonely, she drew near and opened a conversation.

Mrs. Sims responded readily.

"Do sit down, Miss," she said, making room for Mildred by her side. "I'm so glad to 'ave someone to speak to. I gets hawful 'omesick at times."

"Ah, that must be a very trying feeling," Mildred said compassionately. "I know nothing of it myself; for I've never been away from my home or mother for even a week at a time."

"Well, Miss, you're fortunate."

"Have you been long in this country?"

"It's barely six months, Miss, since I left me father's 'ouse in London. We kept an 'otel there, an' that's 'ow I came to know Mr. Sims. He was takin' lodgin' with us while up to London about some business 'e 'ad with the lawyers."

"And are your own family all still in England?"

"Yes, Miss, hevery one. I left 'em all—father, mother, brothers, and sisters—for 'im," she answered with a tremble in her voice, wiping her eyes furtively.

"What a shame he should treat you as he does!" was the indignant exclamation that rose to Mildred's lips. But she checked herself in time and changed it to, "Then I think he ought to be very good to you."

"I 'ope we'll be 'appy, Miss, when we're settled down in a 'ome of our own," remarked the little woman with a half-stifled, patient sigh. "Indeed, it's not 'alf so bad as I expected. I've been hastonished at finding so many white women in America. I thought when I landed in New York, I'd be the honly white woman there. I s'posed all the rest would be fearsome natives."

"Indeed! How relieved you must have been on discovering your mistake," remarked Mildred demurely, while her eyes twinkled with suppressed fun.

"That I was, Miss, as you may well believe. It quite reconciled me to the country."

⚜ ⚜ ⚜

The sun rose brightly the next morning, and the young Keiths were early on deck, romping and racing about full of the vivacity and mirth usually indicative of extreme youth and perfect health.

They were well watched over by their father, Mildred, and Rupert, or there is no knowing what wild and dangerous pranks might have been indulged in by Cyril and Don.

The former actually proposed a flying leap from the deck of the *Queen Charlotte* to that of the steamer and was not at all pleased by the decided veto put upon it by his father.

"I think you might let a fellow try, papa," he grumbled. "It would be such fun, and I know I could do it."

"No, you couldna," said Don, peeping over the ship's side. "It's a big, big space."

"Come over to the other side of the deck and stay there," said Mr. Keith, leading them away.

Rupert followed, holding Fan by the hand. "What was that? What were they throwing in?" he asked, stopping suddenly at a sound as of a heavy body plunging into the water struck his ear, while at the same instant, a startled cry came from the deck of the *Milwaukee*.

"A man overboard!"

"A man overboard!" the fearful cry was taken up and repeated on all sides amid the rush of many feet and the quick, sharp imperative words of command.

Almost instantly, a boat was lowered, and strong arms were pulling with swift, vigorous strokes for the spot already left far behind, where the splash of the falling body had been heard. Keen eyes were eagerly searching the waste of waters. The crews and passengers of the three vessels were crowding the decks and following their movements in breathless anxiety and suspense.

They pulled backward and forward, calling out to the drowning one that help was near.

"Ah, yonder he is at last!" cried a woman's voice in exultant tones. "There he is with his head above water, for I see his hat."

"And they see him, too, and are pulling toward him with all their might!"

"Ah, they're up with him! They have him now! Hurrah!" And a wild cheer rose from the hundreds of throats along the rails.

But it died away in a groan.

"It was his hat—only his hat, poor fellow, and they've given it up and are coming back without him!" sighed the woman who had been the first to raise the alarm.

Every face wore a look of sadness for the few moments of waiting as the rowers slowly returned.

They gained the deck of the *Milwaukee,* and one of them—a lad of nineteen or twenty and a rough, hardy sailor—came forward with a subdued manner in strange contrast to his accustomed rude hilarity, his lips white and quivering and sad tears in his manly eyes.

"Mother, mother," he said, low and huskily, drawing near the woman with tottering steps. "Don't— don't take it too hard. I—I couldn't bear to see you. I did my best. We all did, but we couldn't find him. Here's his hat. It—it was little Billy."

"My boy! Mine! My little one!" she shrieked, and she fell fainting into the arms of her older son.

There was not a dry eye among the spectators, and as the sad story spread to the other vessels, many a tremulous tone and falling tear attested the pity and sympathy of those who told the tale and those who listened to it.

"But how did it happen?" queried one and another. The answer was, "He was jumping back and forth from one vessel to another, and he fell in between the *Milwaukee* and the steamer. It is conjectured that he must have been struck by the wheel, as he did not come up again."

"And it might have been one of ours," sobbed Mrs. Keith, clasping her babe to her breast, while her eyes glanced from one to another of her darlings. "Ah, how frightened I was when I heard the cry. I don't know how I got up the cabin steps! For I thought it was perhaps—"

Tears choked her utterance, tears of mingled gratitude for herself and sorrow for the bereaved mother.

"Yes, it might have been you, Cyril or Don. Think how poor mother's heart would have been broken, and mine, too," Mr. Keith added, sitting down and taking one on each knee. "Now, do you want to try jumping across like that boy did?"

They shook their heads, gazing up into his face with awestruck countenances.

The sad event of the morning seemed to have exerted a subduing influence upon all of the passengers. It was a very quiet day on board.

*❦ ❦ ❦*

The calm continued throughout the day, but a breeze sprang up during the night, and the vessels parted company.

By daylight, the breeze had stiffened into a wind that made the lake very rough. The ship tossed about on the waves with a motion by no means agreeable to the landlubbers in her cabins and steerage. Everything not made fast to the floor or walls went dashing and rolling from side to side of state-room or salon. Few of the passengers cared for breakfast, and those who made the attempt had to do so under serious difficulties, table and floor being both inclined planes, sloping now in one direction, now in another.

They passed a rather miserable day confined to the cabin, for the rain was falling heavily and the great waves would now and then sweep across the deck.

Still, the captain assured them the storm was not a bad one, and they were in no danger.

By the next day, it had abated so that they could seek the outer air, going about without experiencing much difficulty in preserving their center of gravity. Nearly every one had so far recovered from their seasickness as to be able to appear at meals.

Life aboard ship that had seemed quite dreadful during the long hours of the storm became more tolerable.

The older people promenaded the deck, sat there with book or work, or merely chatted, looking out upon the restless waters, while the children amused themselves with their play or in running about exploring every nook and cranny and making acquaintance with the sailors, who seemed to enjoy their innocent prattle and merry ways.

All the Keiths had suffered from seasickness, and Mildred was among the last to recover. It was not until toward sunset of the second day that she could be induced to leave her berth and allow her father to assist her up the cabin stairs to the deck.

Here a couch had been prepared for her, and the loving hands of mother and aunt busied themselves in making her comfortable. Brothers and sisters gathered rejoicingly around. Mrs. Jones brought a glass of lemonade, Mrs. Sims offered smelling salts, someone else a fan, and presently the two captains and the younger Wells came up to offer their congratulations on her recovery.

Then Cyril and Don led up and introduced Mr. Carr, the bachelor gentleman with whom they had already formed a firm friendship.

"He's a real nice man, Milly," said Cyril. "He knows lots of stories and games and things, and—"

"An' p'ays wis us children," put in Don. "And he tan do everyfing."

"Yes, he's weal dood," chimed in Fan. "I likes him."

"Thank you, my little maid," said the gentleman, laughing and stroking her curls. "Now, if you could just get your sister to look at me through your spectacles."

"Why, I hasn't dot any 'pectacles!" exclaimed the child, opening her eyes very wide "Maybe papa buy me some when I dets to be an old lady. Den I lets Milly 'ook froo."

"That's my good, generous little sister," Mildred said, laughing. "If I'm so fortunate as to get glasses first, you shall borrow them whenever you wish."

"Now go to your play, dear, and let sister rest till she feels better," said their mother.

"Please tum wis us, Mr. Tarr," said Don, tugging at that gentleman's coat.

"Don, Don, you must not—"

"Ah, don't reprove him," gently interposed the gentleman, lifting the child to his shoulder and prancing away with him, while the little fellow shouted with laughter and delight.

"Isn't he a nice man?" cried Zillah, and Ada, looking after him, added, "We all like him ever so much."

"Yes," assented the mother, "but I am very much afraid my children impose upon his good nature."

"Don't let that trouble you, Mrs. Keith. He is surely able to take care of himself. Besides, it's quite evident that he enjoys their society as much as they do his," said Edward Wells, taking a seat near Mildred's couch, where he remained chatting in a lively strain with her and the other ladies until it was time for them to retire to the cabin.

Fair weather and favorable winds made the remaining days of the voyage a pleasure till one bright June morning they entered the Straits of Mackinaw, and reaching the island of the same name, they anchored in front of its fort.

The captain, informing the passengers that the ship would lie there for a day or two, good-naturedly offered to take ashore any or all who would like to go.

Nearly everybody eagerly accepted. The boats put off from the ship, each with a full complement of passengers, whom they landed just under the white walls of the fortress situated on a bluff one hundred fifty feet high.

Passing up a flight of stone steps, they entered the parade ground. It was smooth, hard, and clean as a well-swept floor. They walked across and about it, viewing the officers' quarters on the outside and the barracks of the men. They walked along by the wall, noting how it commanded the harbor and the village of Mackinaw with its great guns, beside each of which lay a pile of black balls heaped up in pyramidal form.

Then they visited the town, saw some Indians, and bought curious little bark baskets ornamented with porcupine quills dyed blue, red, and white and filled with maple sugar. They bought moccasins, too, made of soft skins and heavily trimmed with bead work, all made by the Indians.

The young Keiths were made happy with a pair of moccasins apiece from their father, bark baskets from their mother and aunt, and unlimited maple sugar from their friend Mr. Carr.

They returned at last to the ship, tired but full of contentment.

They were as usual early on the deck the next morning, a little before the rising of the sun, for they "liked to see him come up out of the water."

"How very still it is! Hardly a breath of air stirring," Mildred was saying to her father as Edward Wells drew near the little group, all standing together and looking eagerly for the first glimpse of the sun's bright face.

"Yes, we are becalmed," said Mr. Keith.

"Very possibly, we may be detained here for several days in consequence," added Edward, greeting them with a cheerful good morning. "In that case, we will have an opportunity to explore the island. May I have the pleasure of being your guide in so doing?"

"Do you mean all of us?" queried Cyril.

"Yes, my man, if you will all go," answered the sailor lad, but the glance of his eye seemed to extend the invitation to Mildred in particular.

"Oh, father, can we? Can we?" chimed the children in glad chorus.

"We will see," he said. "Now watch, or you'll miss the sight we left our beds so early for."

The matter was under discussion at the breakfast table, and afterward, it was decided that all might go ashore but that the walk under contemplation was too long for the little ones.

Ada Keith was the youngest of that family who was permitted to go, but others joined them, and Edward found himself at the head of quite a party of explorers.

Ada came back looking heated, weary, and troubled. "Oh, mother," she cried with tears in her eyes, "we saw a cave where some Frenchmen were hiding from the Indians and got smoked to death. The Indians did it by building a fire at the cave's mouth, because they couldn't get at them to kill them some other way. Oh, I'm so afraid of the Indians. Do persuade father to take us all back to Ohio again!"

The mother soothed and comforted the frightened child with caresses and assurances of the present peaceable disposition of the Indians. At length, she succeeded in so far banishing her daughter's fears that she was willing to proceed upon her journey.

However, the calm continuing, nearly a week passed and many excursions had been made to the island before they could quit its harbor.

At length one day directly after dinner, a favorable wind having sprung up, the good ship weighed anchor and, pursuing her westward course, she passed out of the straits into Lake Michigan.

All night she flew before the wind, and when our friends awoke the following morning, she rode safely at anchor in the harbor of Chicago.

Though a large city now, it was then a town of less than five thousand inhabitants. This was the final destination port of the *Queen Charlotte,* and her passengers must be landed and her cargo discharged.

It was with feelings of regret on both sides that her officers and the Keiths parted, Edward Wells taking an opportunity to say in an undertone to Mildred that he hoped they would sometime meet again.

St. Joseph, on the opposite side of the lake, was the next port whither the Keiths were bound. A much smaller vessel carried them across.

They had a rough passage, wind and rain compelling them to keep closely housed in a little confined cabin. They were glad to reach the town of St. Joseph, though they found it but a dreary spot— no grass, no trees, and the hotel a large barn-like, two-story building with the hot summer sun streaming in through its windows without hindrance from curtain or blind. The rain had ceased about the time of their arrival, and the sun shone out with fervid heat during the two or three days that they were detained there, resting the Sabbath day and awaiting the arrival of their household goods before ascending the St. Joseph River on which Pleasant Plains, their final destination, was situated.

There were no railroads in that part of the country then, nor for many years after. There was no stage route between the two places, and there were no steamers on the river. The best they could do was to take a keelboat.

The rain had ceased, and the sun shone brightly on the rippling, dancing waters of the lake and river, on the little town, and on the green fields and forests of the adjacent country as they went on board the keelboat *Mary Ann* and set out upon this, the last stage of their long journey.

The boatmen toiled at their oars, and the *Mary Ann* moved slowly on against the current, slowly enough to give our travelers an abundance of time to take in the beauties of the scenery, which they, the older ones at least, did not fail to do.

Much of it was unbroken forest, but they passed sometimes a solitary clearing with its lonely log cabin or sometimes a little village. The river flowed swiftly along, clear and sparkling, between banks now low, now high and green to the water's edge.

The sun was nearing the western horizon as, at last, the boat was run in close to shore and made fast with the announcement, "Here we are, strangers, this here's the town of Pleasant Plains."

# CHAPTER SIXTH

*Nor need we power or splendor,*
*Wide hall or lordly dome;*
*The good, the true, the tender.*
*These form the wealth of home.*

—Mrs. Hall

PLEASANT PLAINS CONSIDERED itself quite a town. It stood high above the river on two plains, the upper familiarly known as the "Bluff." It was laid out in very wide, straight streets, crossing each other at right angles. There were perhaps two hundred dwelling houses, principally frame, but with a goodly proportion of log cabins and a respectable sprinkling of brick buildings.

As the county seat, Pleasant Plains had its own courthouse and jail. There were some half-dozen stores where almost everything could be had—from dress goods to butter and eggs, from a plowshare to a fine cambric needle. There were two taverns, as many blacksmith, shoemaker, and carpenter shops, and a flouring mill and bakery.

There were also two churches belonging to two different denominations. Both were frame structures of extremely plain and unpretentious architecture, with bare walls, uncurtained windows, rough uncarpeted floors, and rude hard benches in lieu of pews.

No thought of architectural beauty or even of comfort and convenience, beyond that of mere protection from the weather, seemed to have entered the minds of any of the builders here. The houses were mere shells, with no cupboards or closets or the slightest attempt at ornamentation.

Nor was their unsightliness concealed by vines, trees, or shrubbery. Almost every one of the beautiful monarchs of the forest once adorning the locality had been ruthlessly felled, and a stump here and there was all that was left to tell of their former existence.

As the keel of the *Mary Ann* grated on the gravelly shore, a tall figure in rough farmer's attire came springing down the bank, calling out in tones of unfeigned joy, "Hello, Keith! Come at last—wife, children, and all, eh? I'm glad to see ye! Never was more delighted in my life."

The speaker, catching Mr. Keith's hand in his, shook it with hearty good will, then, treating the rest of the party in like manner, as with his and Mr. Keith's assistance, each in turn stepped from the boat.

Mr. George Ward was an old client and friend of Mr. Keith's, who had been long urging this removal.

"I declare, I wish I lived in town for a few days now," he went on, "but we're three mile out on the prairie, as you know, Keith. I have my team here, though, and if you'd like to pile into the wagon, all of you, I'll take you home with me, as it is."

The hospitable invitation was declined with grateful thanks.

"There are quite too many of us, Mr. Ward," Mrs. Keith said, smilingly, "and we want to get into a house of our own just as soon as possible."

"Ah, yes, so your husband wrote me, and I've been looking around for you to come. But the best to be had will seem a poor place to you, Mrs. Keith, after what you've left behind in Lansdale."

"I suppose so, but of course we must expect to put up with many inconveniences and probably some hardships, even, for the first few years," she answered cheerfully.

"I'm afraid that's so, but I hope you'll find yourselves paid for it in the long run. Now, shall I take you to the Union Hotel? You can't, of course, get into your own house tonight.

"Here, let me carry you, bub," he said, picking up Cyril. "The soil's real sandy here, and it makes for heavy walking."

"If, as I presume from your recommendation of it, it is your best house of entertainment," Mr. Keith said in reply to the question.

"Yes, sir, there's only one other, and it's a very poor affair," returned Mr. Ward, leading the way.

Mrs. Prior, the landlady, a pleasant-faced, middle-aged woman with kind, motherly manners, met them at the door with a welcome nearly as hearty as that of their old-time friend.

"I'm glad to see you," she said, bustling about to wait upon them. "We've plenty o' room here in town for the right sort o' folks, and we're glad to get 'em."

She had taken them into her parlor, the only one the house afforded.

The furniture was plain—a rag carpet, green paper blinds, a table with a red and black cover, Windsor chairs, two of them rocking chairs with chintz-covered cushions and the rest straight-backed and hard. On the high wooden mantel shelf lay an old-fashioned looking glass, a few shells, and two brass candlesticks. These last were as bright as scouring could make them.

"I'm afraid it must seem but a poor place to you, ladies," she continued, pushing forward a rocking chair for each. "And you're dreadful tired, ain't you, with your long journey? Do sit down and rest yourselves here."

"You are very kind, and everything looks very nice, indeed," Mrs. Keith answered, looking up at her with a pleased smile as she accepted the offered seat and began untying her baby's bonnet strings.

"Indeed, I, for one, didn't expect to find half as good an accommodation out in these western wilds," remarked Aunt Wealthy, glancing around the room. "I thought you had no floors, let alone carpets."

"No floors? Oh, yes, but they are rough to be sure. Carpenters here don't make the best of work, and I think sometimes I could a'most plane a board better myself. But to get the carpets is the rub. We mostly make 'em ourselves, and the weavin's often done so poor that they don't last no time hardly. Soil's sandy, you see, and it cuts the carpets right out."

"They say this country's hard on women and oxen," put in Mr. Ward. "And I'm afraid it's pretty true."

"Now don't be frightening them first thing, Mr. Ward," laughed the landlady. "Come, take off your things and the children's, ladies and make yourselves to home. Here, just let me lay 'em in here," she went on, opening an inner door and revealing a bed covered with a patchwork quilt.

"You can have this room if you like, Mrs. Keith. I s'pose you'd prefer a downstairs one with the baby and t'other little ones? There is a trundle bed underneath that'll do for them.

"And the rest of you can take the two rooms right over these. They're all ready, and you can go right up to 'em whenever you like. Is there anything more I can do for you now?"

The query was answered in the negative.

"Then, I'll just excuse myself," she said. "I must go and see to supper. Can't trust girls here."

She passed out through another door, leaving it ajar.

"That's the dining room, I know, Fan, 'cause I see two big tables set," whispered Cyril, peeping in. "There's not a bit of carpet on the floor. Guess they're cleanin' house."

"Well, wife, I'll have to leave you for a little. I must see to the landing of our goods," said Mr. Keith, taking his hat. "Will you go along, Ward?"

"And let us go up and look at our rooms, girls," said Mildred to her sisters. "Mayn't we, mother?"

"Yes, go and make yourselves nice and neat for the supper table."

They came back reporting bare floors everywhere made of boards none too well planed, either, but everything scrupulously clean.

"Then we may well be content," said their mother. The gentlemen returned, and the guests were presently summoned by the ringing of a bell on top of the house to the supper table, which they found furnished with an abundance of good, wholesome, well-cooked food.

They were really able to make a very comfortable meal, despite the presence of delftware, two-pronged, steel forks, and the absence of napkins.

"What about the goods, Stuart?" asked Mrs. Keith on their return to the parlor.

"I have had them carted directly to the house. That is, I believe the men are at it now."

"The house?"

"The one Ward spoke of. I have taken it. It was Hobson's choice, my dear, or you should have seen it first."

"Can I see it now?"

"Why, yes, if you choose. It won't be dark yet for an hour. If you and Aunt Wealthy will put on your bonnets, I'll take you around."

"Ada and me, too, father?" cried Zillah eagerly.

"And Fan and Don and me?" chorused Cyril.

"You couldn't think of going without your eldest son," said Rupert, looking about for his hat.

Mrs. Keith turned an soft, inquiring eye upon her husband.

"Is it far?"

"No, even Fan can easily walk it. Let them come. You, too, Mildred," she said, taking the babe from her arms. "I'll carry the baby."

"We'll make quite a procession," laughed the young girl. "Won't people stare?"

"What if they do? Who of us cares?"

"Not I!" cried Rupert, stepping back from the doorway with a commanding wave of the hand. "The procession will please move forward, Mr. Keith and his wife taking the lead, Miss Stanhope and Miss Keith next, Zillah and Ada following close upon their heels, the three inseparables after them, with Marshal Rupert bringing up the rear to see that all are in line."

Everybody laughed at this sally while they promptly fell into line as directed, moved out upon the sidewalk, and pursued their way through the quiet streets.

To be sure, people did stare from open doors and windows, some asking, "Who are they?" Others answered, "Newcomers, and they've got a big family to support."

Some remarked that they were nice-looking people. Others shook their heads wisely, or dubiously, and said they "expected they were real stuck-up folks—dressed so dreadfully fine."

However, the subjects of these charitable comments did not overhear them and therefore were not at all disturbed by them.

"Do you see that yellow frame yonder, wife?" Mr. Keith asked as they turned a corner.

"With the gable-end to the street and two doors in it, one above and one below?"

"The same."

"It looks like a warehouse."

"That's what it was originally intended for, but finding it not available for that purpose, the owner offered it for rent."

"And is it the one you have rented?"

"Yes, it is a poor place to take you to, my dear. But, as I told you, it was Hobson's choice."

"Then we'll make the best of it and be thankful."

"What a horrid old thing!" remarked Mildred in an undertone heard only by Aunt Wealthy.

"We'll hope to find the inside an improvement on the out," was the cheerful rejoinder.

"It has need to be, I should say!" cried the girl as they drew near. "Just see! It fronts on two streets, and there's not a bit of a space separating it from either. And the doors open right out onto a sand bank."

"That's what was made by digging the cellar," said Rupert.

"There's a rather big yard at the side and behind," said Zillah.

"Something green in it, too," added Ada, whose sight was imperfect.

"Nothing but a crop of ugly weeds," said Mildred, ready to cry as memory brought vividly before her the home they had left, with its big garden carpeted with green grass and adorned with shrubbery and filled with the bloom of summer flowers.

The June roses must be out now and the wood-bine—the air sweet with their delicious perfume—and they who had planted and tended them were now so far away in this desolate-looking spot.

"Not a tree, a shrub, a flower, or a blade of grass!" she went on, sighing as she spoke.

"Never mind, we'll have lots of them next year, if I have to plant every one myself," said Rupert.

The last load of their household goods had just been brought up from the river, and the men were carrying in the heavy boxes and setting them down upon the floor of the front room. The door stood wide open, and they all walked in.

"Not a bit of a hall!" exclaimed Mildred. "Not a cupboard or closet—nothing but four bare walls and two windows on each side of the front door."

"Yes, the floor and ceilings," corrected Rupert.

"And another door on the other side," said Ada, running and opening it.

"Not a mantelpiece to set anything on, nor any chimney at all! How on earth are we going to keep warm in the wintertime?" Mildred went on, ignoring the remarks of her younger brother and sister.

"With a stove, Miss. Pipes run up through the floor into the room above. There's a flue there," said one of the men, wiping the perspiration from his forehead with the sleeve of his checked shirt.

Mr. Keith stopped to settle with the men for their work, and the others walked on into the next room.

It was as bare and more dreary than the first. It was somewhat larger, but it had only one window and an outside door, which opened directly upon the side street.

In back of the two rooms and in a line with them was the kitchen. It was smaller than either of the other rooms, but it had a chimney, a fireplace, and a small, dark closet under a flight of steep and crooked stairs which led from it to the story above.

This, as they found on climbing up to it, consisted of two rooms, the first extending over kitchen and sitting room, the other over the front room and of exactly the same size.

The stairs led directly into the first room, and it must be passed through to reach the second. Therefore, it had not the least bit of privacy.

"What a house!" grumbled the children. "How will we ever live in it? Only a few rooms and not a bit nice."

Mrs. Keith stood in the middle of that large, barn-like upper room, saying not a word, but with her heart sinking lower and lower as she glanced from side to side, taking in the whole situation.

Aunt Wealthy saw it and came to the rescue. "Never mind, dearie. It will look very different when we have unpacked and arranged your furniture. With the help of curtains, several rooms can be made out of this, and we'll do nicely."

"Yes, no doubt we shall, auntie," Mrs. Keith answered with determined cheerfulness. "That front room shall be yours—"

"No, no! You and Stuart must take that—"

"I'm set on having my own way in this," interrupted the younger lady in her turn. "It is the best room, and you must take it. Don't hesitate or object, for I should be afraid to have my little ones in there with that outside door opening onto nothing," she concluded with a laugh.

"Well, wife, what do you think?" asked Mr. Keith, coming up the stairs.

"That we can be very happy here if we make up our minds to be content with our lot."

"That is like you, Marcia, always ready to make the best of everything," he said with a pleased look.

"I think it is a dreadful place!" exclaimed Mildred. "It is very much like a great barn, and it is so dirty! Plaster all over the floor and spattered on all of the windows, too."

"I hope it can be cleaned," her father said, laughing at her rueful face. "Mrs. Prior can probably tell us where to find a woman to do it."

A little more time was spent in discussing plans for the arrangement of the inside of the dwelling; then they stepped into the side yard and viewed it from the outside.

A great dead wall of rough-weather boarding broken by one window only, and that in the second story, was what met their view as they looked up. Down below was first a heap of sand and beyond that a wilderness of weeds and brushwood.

"I'm dumb with despair!" cried Mildred, folding her hands with a tragical air.

"Can dumb folks talk?" asked Cyril.

"As ugly as mud this side," remarked Zillah, turning up her nose scornfully as she scanned the unsightly wall.

"We'll cover it with vines," said Aunt Wealthy.

"And I'll clear the yard and sod it," added Rupert, seizing a great mullein stalk and pulling it up by the roots as he spoke. "'Twon't be nearly as hard as the clearing the early pioneers of Ohio had to do, our grandfathers among the rest."

"That's the right way to look at it, my boy," responded Mr. Keith heartily. "Come now, we'll lock up the house and go back to our hotel for the night."

"There's a log house nearly opposite," remarked Rupert when they were in the street again, "and the next is a real shabby one-and-a-half-story frame with a blacksmith shop attached. We haven't the worst place in town after all. Ho! Look at the sign, 'G. Lightcap.' What a name! 'Specially for a blacksmith."

Mrs. Prior joined her guests in the parlor after the younger ones had gone to bed.

"Well, how did you like the house?" she asked.

"I hope we shall be able to make ourselves quite comfortable there," Mr. Keith answered in a cheerful tone.

"You can get possession right away, I s'pose."

"Yes, and we do want to move in as quickly as possible but must have some cleaning done first."

Mrs. Prior recommended a woman for that without waiting to be asked, and she offered to "send round" at once and see if she could be engaged for the next day.

The offer was accepted with thanks, and the messenger brought back word that Mrs. Rood would be at the house by six o'clock in the morning.

"But," suggested Aunt Wealthy in dismay, "she'll want hot water, soap, cloths, scrubbing brushes!"

"I'll send a big iron kettle to heat the water," said the landlady. "A fire can be made in that kitchen fireplace, you know, or outdoors, with the brushwood."

"And brushes and soap can be had at the stores, I presume," suggested Mr. Keith.

"Yes, and if they ain't open in time, I'll lend mine for her to start with."

"Thank you very much," said Mrs. Keith. "But, Stuart, we may as well unpack our own. I can tell you just which box to open."

"What a woman you are for doing things so systematically, Marcia," he said admiringly. "Yours is the best plan, I think. Can we be up in time to be on hand there at half past five, think you?"

"We can try," she answered brightly. "Mrs. Prior, where is your market?"

"We haven't got to that yet, ma'am," replied the landlady, laughing and shaking her head.

"No market? Why how do you manage without?"

"There are butcher shops where we can buy fresh meat once or twice a week—beef, veal, mutton, lamb, whatever they happen to kill. And we put up our own salt pork, hams, dried beef, and so forth, and we keep codfish and mackerel on hand.

"Most folks have their own chickens, and the country people bring 'em in, too, and butter and eggs and vegetables, though a good many town folks have gardens of their own, keep a cow, and make their own butter."

"That's the most independent way," remarked Mr. Keith. "I think I must have a cow, if I can get a girl who can milk. Do you know of a good girl wanting a place, Mrs. Prior?"

"I wish I did, but they're dreadful scarce, sir, and so sassy! You can't keep 'em unless you let 'em come to the table with the family, and you must be mighty careful what you ask 'em to do."

# CHAPTER SEVENTH

*I feel my sinews slacken'd with the fright,*
*And a cold sweat thrills down all o'er my limbs,*
*As if I were dissolving into water.*

—DRYDEN'S *TEMPEST*

THE LIGHTCAPS WERE at supper—father and eldest son, each of whom stood six feet in his stockings, with shirt sleeves rolled up above their elbows displaying brown sinewy arms, and the mother in a faded calico, grizzled hair drawn straight back from a dull, careworn face and gathered into a little knot behind, in which was stuck a yellow horn comb. Years of incessant toil and frequent exposure to sun and wind had not improved a naturally dark, rough skin, and there was no attempt at adornment in her attire, not a collar or a ruffle to cover up the unsightliness of the yellow, wrinkled neck.

Rhoda Jane, the eldest daughter, seated at her father's right hand, was a facsimile of what the mother had been in her girlhood, with perhaps an added touch of intelligence and a somewhat more bold and forward manner.

There were also several younger children of both sexes, quite ordinary looking creatures and just now wholly taken up with the business at hand: vying with each other in the amount of bread and butter and molasses, fried potatoes, and fried pork they could devour in a given space of time.

"Some newcomers in town, mother," remarked Mr. Lightcap, helping himself to a second slice of pork. "The keelboat *Mary Ann* come up the river with a lot of travelers."

"Who, father? Somebody that's going to stay?"

"Yes, that lawyer we heerd was comin', you know. What's his name?"

"Keith," said Rhoda Jane. "I heerd Miss Prior tell Damaris Drybread last Sunday after meetin'. And so they're come, hev they?"

"Yes, I had occasion to go up the street a bit ago and saw George Ward takin' 'em to the Union Hotel. The man hisself and two or three wimmin folks and a lot of young'uns."

"Damaris was wishing there'd be some children," remarked Rhoda Jane. "She wants more scholars."

"It don't foller they'd go to her if there was," put in her brother.

"Oh, now you just shut up, Goto! You never did take no stock in Damaris."

"Nor you neither, Rhoda Jane, 'cept once in a great while just fer contrariness. No, I don't take no shine to Miss Drybread. She's a unmitigated old maid."

"I wish the man had been a doctor and good at curin' the agur," said Mrs. Lightcap, replenishing her husband's cup. "What's up now, Rhoda Jane?" she said as that damsel suddenly pushed back her chair, sprang up, and rushed through the adjoining room to the front door.

"A wagon goin' by filled full of great boxes o' goods," shouted back the girl. "There, they're stoppin' at the yaller house on the corner. Come and look."

The whole family, dropping knives and forks, the children with hands and mouths full, ran pell mell to door and windows to enjoy the sight.

"I wonder what's up, father? Are we goin' to have a new store over there, you think?" queried Mrs. Lightcap, standing on the outer step with her hands on her hips and her gaze turned steadily in the direction of the corner house.

"Dunno, mother. B'lieve I'll jest step over and ask. Come along, Goto. I guess they'd like some help with them thar big boxes."

They were kindhearted, neighborly folk, those early settlers of Pleasant Plains, always ready to lend a helping hand wherever it was needed.

"It's the new lawyer feller's traps," announced Mr. Lightcap, as he and his son rejoined the waiting, expectant wife and children. "He's took the house, and we'll have 'em for neighbors."

There was another rush to the door half an hour later when the Keiths were seen passing on their way to inspect their future abode.

"The prettiest gal I ever seen," remarked Gotobed, gazing admiringly after Mildred's graceful, girlish figure as she walked with her family.

"They certainly look like eastern folks," said his mother. "Won't they wish they'd stayed where they was when they find out how hard 'tis to get help here?"

"Real stuck-up folks, dressed to kill," sneered Rhoda Jane. "Look at the white pantalets on them young'uns! And the girl's got a veil on her bunnit."

"Well, what's the harm?" asked Gotobed. "If you had as pretty a skin, I guess you'd be takin' care of it, too."

"Humph! Beauty that's only skin deep won't last," she said, and with a toss of her head, Miss Lightcap walked into the house in her most dignified style.

For the next ten days, the doings at the corner house and the comings and goings of the Keiths were a source of entertainment and intense interest to their neighbors—the Lightcaps and others. This fact should not be wondered at when we consider the monotony of life in the town at that time—no railroad, no telegraph, no newspaper except those brought by the weekly mail, no magazines, no public library, and very few books in private houses.

Really, the daily small occurrences in their own little world were very nearly all the Pleasant Plainers could find to talk or think about.

And the Keiths, as recent arrivals from a longer-settled part of the country and above many of them on the social scale, were considered worthy of more than ordinary attention. Their dress, their manners, the furnishings of their house, and their style of living were subjects of eager discussion.

The general opinion among the Lightcaps and their set seemed to be that the Keiths were too fine for the place, such remarks as the following being frequently heard:

"Why, would you believe it, they've got a real store carpet in that front room, and a sofy and cheers covered with horsehair cloth and white curtains to the winders and pictures hanging up on the walls."

"And the little girls wears white pantalets. Caliker ones such as our youngsters wears isn't good enough for them."

There were in the town, however, a number of families of educated, refined people who rejoiced in this addition to their society and only waited for the newcomers to get settled into their new home before calling.

Among these, Mrs. Keith and her aunt found several pleasant, congenial companions, and with two or three, the acquaintances soon ripened into a close intimacy and a warm, enduring friendship.

Mildred also soon had more than one young girl crony whom she found as worthy of regard as those she had left behind.

Behind the yellow house was a grove of saplings that became a favorite haunt of the children in their recreation. They would bend down the smaller trees and ride them, climb up into the larger ones and sit among the branches, or build baby houses and play housekeeping underneath, where the shade was thickest.

It was here they spent the warm, sunny days while the older members of the family busied themselves in making the dwelling habitable and the yard neat and orderly.

On the morning after their arrival, Rupert spread a buffalo robe on the ground in the shadiest part of the grove, whereon Zillah and Ada seated themselves with their baby sister, who had been entrusted to their care.

There were many lovely wild flowers springing up here and there, and Cyril, Don, and Fan ran hither and thither gathering them, prattling merrily to each other all the while and now and then, uttering a joyous shout as they came upon some new floral treasure.

"Be careful not to go too far away, children," Zillah called to them.

"No, we won't go far," they answered. Cyril added, "And I'll take care of Fan."

In a little while, they came running back with very full hands.

"See! See," they said, "so many and such pretty ones—blue and white and purple and yellow. There, you take these, and we'll pick some more for ourselves and for mother and Aunt Wealthy. We'll make a big bunch for each of them." And away they ran again.

"Oh, aren't they pretty?" cried Ada. "Let's make a bouquet for mother out of these."

"She won't want two," said Zillah, "'specially just now when she has no place to put them. Let's make wreaths for Annis and Fan."

"Oh, yes!" They began sorting the flowers with eager interest, little Annis pulling at them, too, crowing and chattering in sweet baby fashion.

Suddenly, Zillah gave a great start and laid a trembling hand on Ada's arm. Her face had grown very pale, and there was a look of terror in her large, blue eyes.

Ada turned quickly to see what had caused it, and she was quite as much alarmed on beholding a tall Indian, with rifle in hand, tomahawk and scalping knife in his belt, standing within a few feet of them, evidently regarding them with curiosity.

He wore moccasins and leggings and had a blanket about his shoulders. He wore feathers on his head, too, but there was no war paint on his face.

Behind him was a squaw with a great bark basket full of wild berries slung to her back.

The little girls were too terribly frightened to cry out or speak. They sat there as if turned to stone, while the Indian drew nearer and nearer, still closely followed by his squaw.

Stopping close beside the children, he grunted out a word or two to her, and she slung her bark basket to the ground.

Taking up a double handful of the berries, he poured them into Zillah's lap, saying, "Papoose!"

The squaw restored the basket to its place, and the two walked leisurely away; happily not in the direction of Fan and the boys.

The little girls gazed at each other in blank astonishment, then burst out simultaneously, "Oh, weren't you frightened? I thought he was going to kill us!"

"But wasn't it good of him to give us the berries?"

"Yes, he meant them for baby, but mother doesn't let her have any, so we mustn't give them to her."

"No, but I'll call the children to get some."

"Yes, do."

"Where did you get em?" queried Cyril, devouring his share with zest.

"An Indian gave them to us."

"An Indian? Why, that was like a friend and colation! I shan't be 'fraid of 'em any more."

"I don't know, Cyril," returned Ada with a wise shake of her head, "I'd rather not see 'em even with their berries."

The little feast was just ended when they spied a gentleman passing along the road beyond the grove. He turned and came toward them.

"Good morning," he said pleasantly. "You are Mr. Keith's children, I believe?"

"Yes, sir," answered Zillah.

"I'm glad to see you," he said, shaking hands with them. "I should like to make the acquaintance of your parents. Are they at home in the house yonder?"

"Mother is, sir, but I saw father go away a little while ago."

"Do you think your mother could see me for a moment? My name is Lord."

Cyril opened his eyes wide, gazing up into the gentleman's face with an odd expression of mingled curiosity and astonishment.

"I don't know, sir," answered Zillah. "They're just cleaning house, and—Cyril, run and ask mother."

Away flew the child, into the room where Miss Stanhope and Mrs. Keith were overseeing the opening of boxes and the unpacking of the household gear.

"Mother, mother," he cried breathlessly, "the

Lord's out yonder, and he wants to see you! Can he come in? Shall I bring him?"

"The Lord! What can the child mean?" cried Aunt Wealthy, in her astonishment and perplexity nearly dropping a large china bowl she held in her hand.

Mrs. Keith, too, looked bewildered for a moment, then a sudden light broke over her face. "Yes, bring him in," she said, and turning to her aunt as the child sped on his errand, added, "It must be the minister, auntie. I remember now that Stuart told me his name was Lord."

Mr. Lord, who was a very absent-minded man, came in apologizing for his "neglect in not calling sooner." He had been engaged with his sermon, and the matter had slipped his mind.

"I think you are blaming yourself undeservedly, sir," Mrs. Keith said, giving him her hand with a cordial smile. "We arrived in town only yesterday. Let me introduce you to my aunt, Miss Stanhope."

The two shook hands, and Mr. Lord, seating himself upon a box instead of the chair that had been set for him, sprang up instantly with a hurried exclamation.

A portion of the content of a paper of tacks had been accidentally spilt there.

The ladies were too polite to smile. Mrs. Keith offered the chair again, simply saying, "You will find this a more comfortable seat. Please excuse the disorder we are in." He then plunged into talk about the town and the little church he had recently organized there.

# CHAPTER EIGHTH

*Home is the sphere of harmony and peace,*
*The spot where angels find a resting place,*
*When bearing blessings, they descend to earth.*

—MRS. HALE

CYRIL CAME RUNNING back carrying a covered basket.

"He's gone, girls. He wasn't the Lord at all, only a man. He didn't stay long, I guess 'cause he sat down on some tacks and hurted himself.

"Here's our dinner. Mother says we may eat it out here under the trees, and it'll be as good as a picnic."

"So it will. Let's see what it is," and Zillah took the basket and lifted the lid. "Oh, that's nice! There's buttered biscuits and cold tongue and cheese and gingerbread—lots of it—and even a turnover apiece."

"Isn't our mother good?" cried Ada gratefully. "Did you tell her about the Indian and the berries?"

"Yes, and father was there—he just came home—and he says we needn't be a single bit afraid. They don't kill folks now, and they wouldn't dare hurt us right here in town, even if they wanted to."

"Baby's been fretting a little, 'cause she's hungry, I guess," said Zillah, putting a bit of gingerbread in the little one's hand.

"Yes, mother said we should give her some cake. She'll come directly and take her a while. Now let's begin to eat, for I'm hungry as a big, black bear."

"So am I," piped the small voices of Don and Fan. "But father always asks a blessing first."

"Yes," assented Zillah, stopping short in her distribution of the good things. "And mother does it when he's away, but—" and she glanced from one to the other of the childish but grave faces of the little group.

"I'll do it," said Cyril, closing his merry, blue eyes and folding his chubby hands. "Oh, Lord, we thank thee for the gingerbread and turnovers and—and all the good things. Amen. Now give me mine, Zil," he said, opening his eyes wide and holding out both hands.

"Ladies first, you know," answered his sister. "And we must all spread our handkerchiefs in our laps to keep the greasy crumbs from our clothes."

"Oh, yes. I fordot. Help Ada and Fan and yourself, then Don, too, and me last 'cause we're the gentlemen."

"No, myself last, because that's the way mother does."

"And mother and father always do everything right, commented Ada, beginning upon her sandwich and gingerbread.

They were rosy, healthy children, and their appetites were keen. But they were not selfish or greedy, and the supply of food was more than amply sufficient for all.

They were never stinted but had been taught that

waste was sinful, so the remains of the meal were put carefully by in the basket, which Zillah then hung up on a branch near at hand.

As she did so, the others sent up a glad shout, "Mother's coming!" and sprang forward to meet her, while baby held out her hands with a crow of delight.

"Well, dears, had you plenty of dinner?" Mrs. Keith asked, taking Annis in her arms and sitting down on the buffalo robe while they grouped themselves about her.

"Oh, yes. Yes, indeed! There's some left, and it was very good. Thank you for it, mother."

"You quite deserved it. You have been dear, good children, taking care of yourselves and the baby all morning and not giving any trouble to anybody."

How the young cheeks flushed and the eyes grew bright at these words of commendation from those dear lips. How they loved her for them, and what an increased desire to merit her approbation they felt swelling in their hearts.

She could stay with them only a little while but suggested various amusements—some games they might play and some stories Zillah might relate to the younger ones.

"Are you getting done fast, mother? Can we sleep in our own home tonight?" they asked.

"No, dears. Though the bedroom floors are cleaned, there might be some dampness that would injure us. We will go back to the hotel for our supper and to sleep tonight, but tomorrow night we will be in our own home once more."

"Not the nice home we used to have, though!" sighed Zillah.

"No, daughter, but we must try to be content and thankful. If we are, we may be as happy in the new home as we were in the old."

With that, the now sleeping babe was laid gently down on the robe and a light covering thrown over her. With a charge to the others to take care of her and a caress bestowed upon each, the mother hastened back to the house.

"We're tired of running 'bout and picking flowers, Fan and Don and me," said Cyril. "Won't you please tell us a story now, Zil?"

"Yes, I'll tell you 'Androcles and the Lion.' You always like that."

"Yes, and then tell 'bout the girl that had a silk dress and couldn't run and play cause her shoes pinched," begged Fan.

"Oh, look!" exclaimed Ada in an undertone. "See those girls? They haven't silk dresses or shoes to pinch their toes. Don't they look different?"

The subjects of her remark were two little maids—one about her own size, the other a trifle smaller—who were slowly making their way through the bushes toward the spot where the Keith children were seated.

They had sallow, sunburnt faces and tawny yellow locks straggling over their shoulders. Their thin, lanky little forms were arrayed in calico dresses that were faded, worn, and skimpy, and pantalets of the same material but of a different color appeared below their skirts. Their feet were bare, and on their heads were sunbonnets of pasteboard covered with still another pattern of calico both faded and soiled.

"Shall we ask them to come and join us?" queried Zillah.

"No, they don't look nice. They're dirty, Zil," whispered Cyril with a glance of disgust directed toward the strangers.

"Maybe dey is hungry," suggested Fan. "Let's div 'em somefing out o' de basket."

"Good afternoon, little girls," said Zillah, raising her voice slightly, as they drew near. "Will you come and sit with us?"

They shook their heads but came creeping on, each with a finger in her mouth.

"Have you had your dinner?" An affirmative nod.

"I'm going to tell a story to these children, and if you would like to come and listen, too, you can. What are your names?"

"Mine's Emmaretta Lightcap, and hers is Minerva Lightcap. She's my sister, she is. Now go on and tell your story. Min, let's set down on the grass right here."

They listened in open-mouthed wonder till summoned by a shrill voice from the direction of the smithy, then they rose and scampered away.

The Keiths were a very domestic family. There was no place like home to them, and all, from the father down to little Fan, were heartily weary of the unsettled life they had led for some weeks past.

It was therefore with joy that they found themselves once more able to sit down under their own "vine and fig tree." That is, if a rented domicile so unsightly as "the yellow house on the corner" may fitly be compared to natural objects so full of beauty and grace.

By the evening of the second day, the advanced stage of the internal improvements warranted their taking possession.

As the shadows grew long, the children were called in, and the family gathered about a neatly appointed table set out in the center one of the three lower rooms, which was spoken of indifferently as the sitting, or dining room, since it must serve both purposes.

The meal was enlivened by cheerful chat in which the children were allowed to take part—the only restriction being that one voice was to be heard at a time, and that not in loud or boisterous tones.

No domestic help had been found yet, and leaving mother and aunt to chat with father, Mildred and the younger girls cleared the table, washed the dishes, and made all neat in the kitchen.

This done, they returned to the sitting room. The great family Bible lay open on the table before the father, a pile of hymnbooks beside it. These last Rupert took up and distributed. Mr. Keith read a few verses of Scripture and gave out a hymn. Mrs. Keith's sweet voice set the tune, the others joined in, and a full chorus of praise swelled upon the summer evening air.

It died away, and all knelt while the father offered a short but fervent prayer giving thanks for the mercies of the day, asking for protection through the night, confessing sins, and pleading for pardon and eternal life for all temporal and spiritual good, through the atoning blood of Christ.

It was thus each day was begun and ended in this truly Christian family. "As for me and my house, we will serve the Lord," was the resolution with which Mr. and Mrs. Keith had begun their married life.

Each little one came to claim a goodnight kiss from their father and Aunt Wealthy, then cheerfully followed their mother up the steep and crooked stairway to the large room above.

"Oh, how much nicer it looks! Auntie's room, too," they cried, running to the open door and peeping in.

Everything was now clean and neat. Carpets covered the rough boards of the floor, and curtains draped the windows and divided the large room into several apartments, in each of which was a neat, white bed.

Little of their heavy furniture had been brought with them from the old home, but its place was partially supplied by turning packing boxes into chintz-covered and cushioned lounges and dressing tables, whose unsightliness was concealed by dainty drapery. Ingenuity and taste had done wonders in making the house comfortable and attractive at very small expense.

# CHAPTER NINTH

*'Tis necessity,*
*To which the gods must yield.*

THE CHILDREN HAD said their prayers, tired little heads were laid on soft white pillows, weary young limbs stretched out to rest, and leaving a kiss on each rosy mouth, the mother went downstairs to rejoin her husband and aunt in the sitting room.

She found Mrs. Prior with them. The good woman had "just run in" to tell them of a girl in want of a place.

"I don't know anything about her," she went on, "except that she's a right decent-looking girl and wants to work out a spell. They tell me the family's English—respectable but poor.

"If you would wish to give her a trial, Mis' Keith, I've an opportunity to send her word this evening. Like as not, she'd get a chance to come in with some of the country folks tomorrow."

Mrs. Keith gladly gave consent, feeling as if almost any sort of help would be better than none. Then she asked, "Is there any school in town that you could recommend for my little girls, Mrs. Prior?"

"Well, I don't know of but one, and I've my doubts about that bein' such as you'd want to send 'em to.

Damaris Drybread's the teacher, and I shouldn't judge by her talk that she'd had a finished education—not by no means! Still, she may do well enough for little ones. I haven't any, so I haven't tried her."

"Suppose we have a light," suggested Mr. Keith. "It's growing too dark for us to see each other's faces."

Mildred rose, went to the kitchen, and presently returned with a lighted candle and a pair of snuffers, which she placed on the table.

Miss Stanhope was asking what sort of society was to be found in the place, to which Mrs. Prior made answer, "Well, ma'am, we have pretty much all sorts and don't divide up in circles like they do in a good many places. I s'pose there'll be more of that as the town grows larger.

"There's educated folks that's fond o' books and the like and know what manners is and how to talk well. There's others that's rough and ignorant, yet mostly well-meaning with it all—real honest and industrious.

"There are very few thieves, if any. Folks leave their doors unlocked—sometimes wide open—at night, their clothes hanging out on the line, and I never hear of anything bein' took. There's very little drinking, either. A drunken man's a rare sight with us."

"There are a good many New Englanders here, are there not?" inquired Mr. Keith.

"Yes, quite a good many from New York state and Pennsylvany and Virginia—from Jersey, too. I hail from there myself.

"But I must be going now. It's gettin' late. Evenings is so short this time o' the year, and however it may be with Mr. Keith, I know you women folks are tired enough to be ready for bed.

"Now don't be formal with me but run in whenever you can. I'll always be glad to see you.

"No, never mind your hat, Mr. Keith. I don't want an escort, for I'm not the least mite afraid. Goodnight to you all," she said and hurried away.

The candle was flaring and wasting in the wind. Miss Stanhope hastened to snuff it, remarking, "These are miserable tallows. Get me some candle wax tomorrow, Stuart, and I'll try to make some that will be an improvement upon them. We have the molds and the wick. All we lack is the tallow."

Near noon the next day, a flauntily dressed young woman walked in the open door and introduced herself to Mrs. Keith as the "Hinglish girl, Viny Apple, that Mrs. Prior had recommended."

Mrs. Keith received her kindly. "Can you cook and do general housework?" she asked.

"Yes, mum, of course. That's what I came for."

"I hope you understand how to work, but it is not to be expected that your way will always be what will suit me best. So, I trust you are willing to be directed somewhat."

"If you're not too hard to please. I'll suit, I'm sure."

"Then we will try it. Zillah, show Viny where she is to sleep."

"Is she to come to the table?" asked Mildred when the two had disappeared up the stairway.

"We shall see. I have not spoken of it yet."

"You won't put up with that, mother, surely?"

"I think I must if it is the only condition on which we can have help with our housework."

On coming down, Viny was directed to set the table for dinner. She was shown where to find the requisite articles, told how many were in the family, and left to the performance of her task.

Mildred noted the number of plates set on and saw that Viny had counted herself in with the rest.

"You have one plate too many," she said with some sharpness of tone.

"No, Miss."

"You certainly have. Here are eleven, and we are only ten."

"And I make 'leven," returned Viny with a hot flush on her cheek and an angry gleam in her eyes.

"You?"

"Yes, Miss, I'm as good as the rest, and if I cook victuals, I 'ave a right to eat 'em."

A warning glance from her mother's eye checked the angry exclamation on the tip of Mildred's tongue.

"We will consent to your coming to the table with us, Viny, on condition that you are always neat and tidy in appearance," Mrs. Keith remarked in a quiet tone. "And now you may help me dish up the dinner."

Aunt Wealthy was busy with her candle molds in one corner of the kitchen, putting in the wicks.

"So that question's settled," she said in an aside to her niece. "I think you have done wisely, Marcia."

The faces that surrounded the dinner table that day were a study. Those of Miss Stanhope and Mrs. Keith wore their usual placid expressions, but

Mildred's was flushed and angry, Rupert's full of astonishment, reflected to some extent by the younger ones, while that of the newcomer expressed self-assertion and defiance.

Mr. Keith glanced quizzically from one to another for a moment, then gave his attention to filling the plates, talking at the same time in a cheerful strain.

"I have found a lot, wife, which I think will suit us for building on. If nobody feels too tired for a walk after tea, we will all go and look at it. It is to be for the family, and the family must decide as to its merits."

This turned the current of thought, and all the young people grew eager and animated. It was quite evident that no one intended to be too much fatigued to be of the party of inspection.

In the midst of the talk, a half-terrified exclamation from Fan drew attention of all. Following the direction of her glance, they saw a tall Indian in the doorway, and in the street were many others, some on foot, some on horseback, some in the act of dismounting.

They were of both sexes and all ages. The papooses were tied into little wooden troughs, which the mothers stood up on end on the ground.

The babies were very quiet, not a whimper to be heard. They were deprived of the use of their hands— their clothing being a straight strip of cloth folded around their bodies in such a way as to pin their poor little arms down to their sides—and had nothing to amuse them but a string of tiny bells stretched across the trough in front of their faces.

"Ugh!" said the Indian on the doorstep. "Shawp!"

and he pointed from a basket of berries his squaw had set down beside him to the loaf on the table.

"Oh, do let's give it to 'im! No knowin' what 'e'll do if we don't!" cried Viny in a fright.

"It will be a good exchange," said Mr. Keith, taking the loaf and handing it to the Indian. "Bring a pan for the berries."

The Indian passed the loaf to his squaw with a grunt of satisfaction, poured a quart or so of berries into the pan Viny brought, then again pointed to the table.

"What now?" asked Mr. Keith, good-humoredly.

The Indian replied by a gesture, as if lifting a cup to his lips. "He's thirsty," Mildred said as she hastened to pour out a tumbler of milk and hand it to him.

He drank it, returned the glass with a nod of thanks, and walked away.

"I'll just run hout and water 'em hall," said Viny, hurrying into the kitchen for a bucket and a tin cup. "It's always best to keep on the good side of 'em, folks tell me, if you don't want to run the risk of losin' the 'air hoff yer 'ead."

Mr. Keith was standing in the doorway where the Indians had been a moment before.

"Come look at them, wife, and all of you," he said. "It's quite a show, and there's not the least danger."

Thus encouraged, the children crowded to the door and window and found much amusement in watching the movement of the savages and Viny's efforts to win favor with them.

Her efforts were apparently well-directed, for the day was warm, and they drank the cool water freshly drawn from the well in the yard as if they found it very refreshing.

The troop—some thirty or forty in number—did not tarry long. In less than an hour, they had all remounted and gone on their way.

"There! Them Hinjuns is all clear gone, and hour scalps is safe for the present," remarked Viny with a sigh of relief as the last one disappeared from view in a cloud of dust far down the street.

She had run out to the corner of the house, dish-towel in hand, to watch their movements.

"Don't talk so. You'll frighten the children," said Mildred, speaking from the front door where she stood with the little ones grouped round about her.

"I don't take horders from you," muttered the girl, stalking back to the kitchen.

After tea, the proposed family walk was taken.

The lot, farther north of town than any built upon yet and situated on the high riverbank overlooking the ferry, was pronounced all that could be desired.

It was on a corner, and two sides afforded a fine view of the river, while the others offered views of town and country.

"When we have our house built," remarked Mr. Keith, "we'll be able to see the Kankakee Marsh from the second-story windows."

"Marsh?" repeated his wife in a tone of alarm, "How far off is it?"

"We're about two miles from this end. It is two hundred miles long, you remember, extending far over into Illinois. But why that sigh?"

"Ague!"

"Well, don't let us cross the bridge before we come to it. This is a beautiful spot. I think we can, in a few years, make it superior in regard to beauty as any we have ever lived in."

"I think so, too, if we can keep these fine old oaks."

There were several of them—grand, old trees that had stood the storms of centuries, perhaps.

"We will. We'll manage our building in a way not to interfere with them."

At that, Mildred's face brightened as it had not since her first sight of the yellow house.

She had been very homesick for the dear old home in Lansdale, though not a word of it had she breathed even into her mother's sympathetic ear.

"How soon can the house be done?" she asked.

"Better inquire first how soon it will be begun," laughed her father. "If we get into it by next spring, we may consider ourselves fortunate."

"Oh dear!" sighed the children with one accord.

"We'll soon get the ground fenced in and let you spend your leisure time there and exercise your good taste and ingenuity in beautifying it," said their father.

"May we all help plan the house?" asked Rupert.

Mr. Keith smiled a kindly, good-natured smile with some amusement in it, too.

"You may all make suggestions. It is to be *our* home—not the parents' only, but the children's, too."

# Chapter Tenth

*Heaven gives us friends to bless the present scene.*

—Young

"Oh, Rhody Jane, Rhody Jane, I say, just come an' look!"

"Look at what, Emmaret? You're always makin' a fuss about nothin'," returned Miss Lightcap scornfully, but nevertheless stepping very promptly, plate and dishcloth in hand, to the front door from whence the hasty summons had come.

"'Tain't nothin' this time," Emmaretta went on. "They're agoin' to Sunday school, them Keith girls, and just see how they're dressed up!"

"Did you ever see anything so fine?" added Minerva. "Sech lovely dresses and black silk aprons with colored lace onto 'em. Oh my! I wish I had one like 'em!"

"Maybe you shall some o' these days when your pop gits rich," said her mother, who was gazing from the window.

"But the bonnets is what takes me. Did you notice 'em, Rhoda Jane? They're gimp, with blue ribbings and blue flowers."

"And the white and red in their faces makes them powerful becoming," said Gotobed, standing outside.

But he turned his head the other way, rather shamefacedly, as Mildred, looking sweet and fair in white muslin and pink ribbons, followed her younger sisters into the street and sent a casual glance in his direction.

"Don't she think she's something!" said Rhoda Jane quite enviously.

"And so she is. She looks like a posy," said Gotobed.

"Is that the grandmother, the old lady walking with Mr. Keith?"

"No, Viny Apple says she's Mrs. Keith's aunt and talks in the funniest way sometimes—gets things hind part before—telling her to make up the floors and sweep the beds and the like.

"There, they're all out o' sight. I guess the mother's staying home with the baby. Viny said she wasn't agoin', too, and I s'pose she's upstairs primpin'.'"

"And that's what you'd ought to be doin' before long, if you're going to meetin', Rhoda Jane," observed Mrs. Lightcap, drawing in her head. "Hurry up now with them dishes. And you children walk right in here and hunt up your Sunday things and wash your hands and faces, and comb your hair. It'll be meetin' time 'fore you know it."

A narrow footpath, bordered on each side by grass still wet with dew, led past the grove of saplings to the little church whither the Keiths were bound.

Mildred, lifting her white skirts daintily and

warning her sisters and brothers of the dangers of wet and soiled shoes should they step aside from the beaten track, picked her way with careful steps, rejoicing in the fact that the distance was not great.

The church membership was as yet very small; Sabbath school ditto. The newly arrived family made an important addition to the ranks of both teachers and scholars.

Two Bible classes were organized this morning and given, respectively, into the charge of Mr. Keith and Miss Stanhope—Rupert becoming a member of his father's and Mildred of Aunt Wealthy's. There were but two others in this latter class: Claudina Chetwood and Lucilla Grange, both intelligent, ladylike, refined girls, who made an agreeable impression upon Miss Stanhope and Mildred also. And the feeling was mutual.

The morning service followed immediately upon the close of Sabbath school. The sermon was excellent, and the singing, though not artistic and somewhat interrupted by the necessity of lining out the hymn on account of the scarcity of books, was earnest and spirited as the people sang apparently with understanding and also from the heart. The prayer was fervent, and the behavior of the congregation throughout the whole service was quiet and devotional.

Most of them were town folk, but a few families had come in from the surrounding country.

There was little display of fashion or style in dress. No one was expensively attired, and most of the women and girls wore calico. But all were neat, some really tasteful, and in intellect and moral worth, the majority of faces would have compared favorably with an equal number in the older States.

People lingered some time after church for mutual introductions and the exchange of friendly remarks and inquiries. The Keiths were warmly welcomed, assured of intentions to call, hopes expressed that they would "like the place" and feel quite at home in the church and be sociable. The country people added, "Come out and see us whenever you can."

Squire Chetwood and Mr. Keith, who had made acquaintance during the preceding week, now introduced their families, each withvery excusable fatherly pride in the good looks and good manners of his offspring.

The young Chetwoods were nearly as numerous and as handsome and intelligent as the Keiths.

"I hope we shall be good friends," said Claudina, as she and Mildred walked away together. "Mother was not out today because of a headache, but she and I are coming to see your mother and you this week."

"We shall be very pleased to see you," Mildred answered heartily, "and I am very glad to accept your offer of friendship."

They parted at Mr. Keith's door, mutually pleased, and Mildred carried a brighter face into the house than she had worn for weeks.

Her mother remarked upon it with delight.

"Yes, mother," she responded merrily, "I begin to feel a little happier about living here, now that I find

we are to have good preaching, Sunday school—
with an excellent and competent teacher for my
share," she said, glancing archly at Aunt Wealthy's
kindly, sensible face, "and pleasant friends." She
went on to give a flattering description of the
Chetwoods, particularly Claudina.

"I hope she will prove a valuable friend and a very
great comfort to you, daughter," said Mrs. Keith.
"You need young companionship, and I am very glad
to know that it will be provided."

The little girls had been upstairs putting away
their bonnets.

"Where's Viny?" asked Zillah, running back into
the sitting room where the older people still were.

"She went out, telling me that she wouldn't be
back until bedtime," replied the mother.

"Leaving us to do our own work!" cried Mildred.
"Oh, mother, what made you let her?"

"Let her, my child? She did not ask my
permission," laughed Mrs. Keith. "But, I think we
are quite as well off without her for today; as we do
no cooking on Sunday."

Before another week had passed, Mildred was
ready to subscribe to the opinion that they were as
well without her altogether—she having proved
herself utterly inefficient, slow, and slovenly about
her work, unwilling to be directed, impertinent,
bold, and forward.

There was not a day when Mildred's indignation
did not rise to fever heat in view of the many and
aggravated sins of omission and commission on the

part of their "help," yet it seldom found vent in words. She was striving with determined purpose to rule her own spirit, asking daily and hourly for strength for the conflict from Him who has said, "In me is thine help," and "My strength is made perfect in weakness."

The example set her by her mother and aunt was also most helpful. They were both cheerful, patient, sunny-tempered women with never a word of fretfulness or complaint from the lips of either. Aunt Wealthy was as calm and serene as an unclouded summer day, while Mrs. Keith often brought to her aid a strong sense of the ludicrous, turning her vexations into occasions for jesting and mirth.

Mildred knew that they were trials nevertheless, and her love and admiration, and her resolve to show herself worthy to be the daughter of such a mother, grew apace.

To the affectionate heart of the unselfish girl there seemed no greater trial than seeing this dear mother overburdened with care and toil, but try as she might to take all the burdens on her young shoulders, it was utterly impossible. And while the conviction that seeing her impatient and unhappy would add to her mother's troubles helped Mildred maintain her self-control, the reflection that Viny's shortcomings added largely to those trials made it tenfold more difficult to bear with them.

So it also was with the little tempers, untidinesses, and mischievous pranks of her younger brothers and sisters.

Home, even a happy home, is often a hard-fought battlefield, and who shall say that there is not sometimes more courage displayed there than in another kind of conflict amid the roar of cannon and clash of arms, where earthly glory and renown are to be won?

The Chetwoods, the Granges, and several others of the same standing in society called that week, among them Mr. Lord, the minister, also brought his old mother who kept house for him, he being a bachelor.

When Viny happened to be the one to admit callers, she seemed to think it incumbent upon her to take a seat in the parlor with them and exert herself for their entertainment.

Mildred speedily undertook to disabuse her of this impression, but the girl haughtily informed her that "she had as good a right in the parlor as anybody else."

"But I wouldn't go into it to visit with anybody that didn't come to see me," said Mildred with a determined effort to keep down her rising anger.

"Well, I guess they're about as likely to want to see me as any o' the rest, and if they don't, they ought to. So there!"

"But you have your work to attend to."

"The work can wait. And the rest o' you's got plenty to do, too."

The only remedy was to keep Viny busy in the kitchen while some of the family watched the doors into the streets and admitted visitors.

Even this stratagem sometimes failed, and they could only console themselves that the visitors understood the situation.

"Ain't you goin' to call on the Keiths?" asked Gotobed Lightcap at the dinner table one day about the middle of the week.

"Who? Me?" queried his mother. Then pushing away her empty plate and resting her elbows on the table with her chin in her hand while she looked reflectively off into vacancy, she added, "Well, I s'pose a body'd ought to be neighborly, and I'm as willin' to do my part as the next one, but there's always a sight of work to do at home, and then I feel kinder backward 'bout callin' on 'em. They live so fine, you know. Viny Apple says they use real silver spoons and eat off real chiney every day, an' that's more'n we can do when we have company."

"Well, old woman, I guess the victuals don't taste no better for bein' eat off them things," responded her husband cheerfully, passing his empty cup.

"Maybe. And they don't have no tea nor coffee for dinner, Viny says. I think it's real stingy."

"P'raps they don't want it," remarked Gotobed.

"Don't you b'lieve no such thing!" exclaimed Rhoda Jane scornfully. "'Tain't fashionable, and they'd rather be fashionable than comfortable. Viny says they're awful stuck up. They wouldn't let her come to the table or into the parlor if they could help themselves.

"But I don't keer. I'm not afeared on 'em, even if mother is. And I'm goin' over there this afternoon —

if it's only to let 'em see that I feel myself as good as they be any day. I'll tell 'em so, too, if they don't treat me right."

"P'shaw, Rhoda Jane, how you talk!" said her mother sharply.

"Well, I'm spunky, mother. That's a fact, and I ain't a bit ashamed of it, nuther."

"Don't you go if you can't behave yourself," said Gotobed, leaving the table and the room.

Mrs. Keith had gathered her children about her in the parlor, it being the shadiest and coolest room in the house in the afternoon. She, herself, Aunt Wealthy, and the little girls were sewing, while Rupert kept the little boys quiet and interested with the making of a kite, and Mildred read aloud from Mrs. Sherwood's *Roxobelle.*

Mildred had a clear, sweet-toned voice, enunciated distinctly, and read with feeling and expression; thus, it was a pleasure to listen to her.

Rupert, Zillah, and Ada were also good readers, and they would take their turns as such, for this was no new thing but one of the mother's ways of educating her children and training them to love literature.

While many another thing had been left behind in Ohio, they had brought all their books with them. Poetry, histories, biographies, books of travel, religious and scientific works, juvenile storybooks, and a few novels, all of the best class, were to be found among their treasured stores and reveled in by old and young.

Mr. Keith had his volumes of legal lore, too, but with these, the other members of the family seldom, if ever, cared to interfere.

Mrs. Sherwood was a favorite author with the young people. They were reading *Roxobelle* for the first time and had reached a most exciting part — the scene where the little dog had led Sophia Beauchamp into the room where his invalid and much-abused mistress lay, chained by disease to her wretched bed, when Mrs. Lightcap and Rhoda Jane appeared in the open doorway.

They were dressed with the utmost simplicity — gowns, aprons, and sunbonnets of calico, made without regard to fashion with no collars or cuffs. Their hands were bare and brown and faces sunburnt. The mother's expression was stolid, the girl's sufficiently sharp but lacking education and refinement.

It was far from being a welcome interruption. Mildred closed her book with a half-suppressed sigh. The little girls exchanged glances of vexation and disappointment. Rupert, too, scowled and uttered an exclamation of impatience half under his breath. But Mrs. Keith and Miss Stanhope rose smilingly, gave the visitors a cordial greeting, asked them to be seated, and entered into conversation.

"It's powerful warm," remarked Mrs. Lightcap, accepting the offered chair and wiping the perspiration from her heated face with the corner of her apron.

"Yes, it has been an unusually warm day," responded Miss Stanhope, handing her a fan, while

Mrs. Keith asked pleasantly if they would not like to take off their bonnets.

"Well, ma'am, I don't care if do," returned Mrs. Lightcap, pulling hers off and laying it in her lap, Rhoda Jane doing likewise.

"Let me lay them on the table," Mildred said, recovering her politeness.

"No thank you. 'Tain't worthwhile fer the few minutes were agoin' to set.

"Our names is Lightcap. This here's my daughter Rhoda Jane, and she says to me 'Mother,' says she, 'we ought to be sociable with them new neighbors of ourn. Let's go over a set a bit.' No, now what am I talkin' about? 'Twasn't her, nuther; 'twas Goto that spoke of it first, but my gal here was more'n willing to come."

"Yes, we always try to be neighborly," assented the girl. "How do you like Pleasant Plains, ladies?"

"It seems a pleasant town, and we find pleasant people in it," was Mrs. Keith's smiling rejoinder.

"That's the talk!" exclaimed Mrs. Lightcap, laughing. "You'll do, Mis' Keith."

"Comin' so late you won't be able to raise no garden sass this year," remarked the mother. Then she went on to give a detailed account of what they had planted, what was growing well, and what was not, with an occasional digression to her husband, her cooking and housework, the occasional attacks of "agur" that interfered with her plans, and so on and so on—her daughter managing to slip in a word or two now and then. At length, they rose to go.

"How's Viny?" queried Rhoda Jane, addressing Mildred directly.

"Quite well, I believe," returned Mildred in a freezing tone, drawing herself up with dignity.

"Tell her we come to see her, too," laughed the girl, as she stepped from the door. "Good-bye. Hope you won't be ceremonious but run in sociable any time o' day."

# CHAPTER ELEVENTH

*Zeal and duty are not slow:*
*But on occasion's forelock watchful wait.*

— MILTON

"THE IMPUDENT THING!" exclaimed Mildred to her mother with a flushed and angry face. "Putting us and our maid of all work on the same level! Visit her? Not I, indeed! And I do hope, mother, that neither you nor Aunt Wealthy will ever cross their threshold."

"My dear, she probably did not mean it," said Mrs. Keith.

"And now let us go on with our story. You have all waited quietly and politely like good children."

"Gotobed Lightcap! Gotobed Lightcap! Gotobed Lightcap!" sang Cyril, tumbling about on the carpet. "Oh, Don, don't you wish you had such a pretty name as that?"

"No, I wouldna. I just be 'Don'."

"There, dears, don't talk now. Sister's going to read," said their mother. "If you don't want to be still and listen, you may run out and play in the yard."

"Somebody else tumin'," whispered Fan, pulling at her mother's skirts.

Mildred closed again the book she had just resumed, rose, and inviting the newcomer to enter, handed her a chair.

She was a tall, gaunt, sallow-complexioned woman of uncertain age, with yellow hair, pale blue eyes, and a sanctimonious expression of countenance.

Her dress was almost austere in its simplicity: a dove-colored calico, cotton gloves of a little darker shade, a white muslin handkerchief crossed on her bosom, and a close straw bonnet with no trimming but a skirt of plain, white ribbon and a piece of the same put straight across the top, brought down over the ears, and tied under her chin.

"My name is Drybread," she announced with a slight, stiff curtsy. Then seating herself bolt upright on Mildred's offered chair, she waited to be addressed.

"Mrs. or Miss?" queried Mrs. Keith pleasantly.

"Miss. And yours?"

"Mrs. Keith. Allow me to introduce my aunt, Miss Stanhope, and my daughter Mildred. These little people, too, belong to me."

"Gueth we do, don't we?" asked Don, showing a double row of pearly teeth. "Cauth you're our own mamma. Ain't she, Cyril?"

"Do you go to school, my little man?" asked the visitor, unbending slightly in the stiffness of her manner.

"Ain't your man! Don't like dwy bread, 'cept when I'se vewy hungwy."

"Neither do I," chimed in Cyril. "And we don't go to school. Papa says we're not big enough, yet."

"Don! Cyril! My little boys must not be rude," reproved the mamma. "Run away now to your play."

"They're pretty children," remarked the caller as the twain disappeared.

"Very frank in the expression of their sentiments and wishes," the mother responded smiling.

"Extremely so, I should say," added Mildred dryly.

"Is it not a mother's duty to curb and restrain?" queried the visitor, fixing her cold blue eyes upon Mrs. Keith's face.

"Certainly, where she deems it needful."

Mrs. Keith's tones were perfectly sweet-tempered, but Mildred's were not quite so as she added with emphasis, "And there is no one so capable of judging when it is needful as my mother."

"Quite natural and proper sentiments for her daughter, no doubt. How do you like Pleasant Plains?"

The question was addressed more particularly to Miss Stanhope, and it was she who replied.

"We are quite disposed to like the place, Miss Stalebread. The streets are widely pleasant and would be quite beautiful if the forest trees had been left."

"My name is *Dry*bread! A good, honest name, if not quite so aristocratic and fine-sounding as Keith."

"Excuse me!" said Miss Stanhope. "I have an unfortunate kind of memory for names and had no intention of miscalling yours."

"Oh! Then it's all right."

"Mrs. Keith, I'm a teacher and take young boys

and girls of all ages. Perhaps you might feel like entrusting me with some of yours. I see you have quite a flock."

"I will take it into consideration," Mrs. Keith answered. "What branches do you teach?"

"Reading, writing, arithmetic, geography, and English grammar."

"I've heard of teachers boarding round," remarked Mildred, assailed by a secret apprehension. "Is that the way you do it?"

"No. I live at home at my father's."

The conversation sallied on for some time before Miss Drybread took her leave.

She was scarcely out of earshot when Ada burst out vehemently.

"I don't want to be distrusted to her! She doesn't look distrusty. Does she, Zillah? Mother, please don't consider it!"

"But just say yes at once?" asked mother playfully, pressing a kiss upon the little flushed, anxious face.

"Oh, no, no, no! Please, mamma," cried the child, returning the caress and putting her arms about her mother's neck. "You didn't like her, did you?"

Mrs. Keith acknowledged laughingly that she had not been very favorably impressed, and Zillah, joining in Ada's entreaties, presently promised that she would try to hear their lessons at home, a decision that was received with delight and a profusion of thanks and caresses.

Mildred was glad to find herself alone with her mother that evening for a short time after the younger ones were in bed, for she had a grand plan to unfold.

It was that she should act as governess to her sisters and the little boys, if they were considered old enough now to begin the ascent of the hill of science.

"My dear child!" the mother said with a look of proud affection into the glowing, animated face. "I fully appreciate the love and self-devotion to me and the children that has prompted this plan of yours, but I am by no means willing to lay such heavy burdens upon your young shoulders."

"But mother—"

"Wait a little, dearie, till I have said my say. Your own studies must be taken up again. Your father is greatly pleased with a new arrangement he has just made for you and Rupert and Zillah to recite to Mr. Lord.

"The English branches, Latin, Greek, and the higher mathematics are what he is willing to undertake to teach."

Mildred's eyes sparkled. "Oh, mother, how glad I am! Will he open a school?"

"No, only hear recitations for a couple of hours every weekday except Saturdays, which he says he must have unbroken for his pulpit preparations.

"Your father thinks he is very glad for the opportunity to add a little to his salary; which, of course, is quite small."

"Then we study at home? I shall like that. But he won't take little ones?"

"No, none that are too young to learn Latin. Your father wants Zillah to begin that now, and he hopes that a few others will join the class—some of the Chetwoods, perhaps."

Mildred's face was all aglow with delight, for she had a great thirst for knowledge, and there had seemed small hope of satisfying it in this little frontier town where the means for acquiring a liberal education were so scant and poor.

"So you see, daughter, you will have no lack of employment," Mrs. Keith went on, "especially as with such inefficient help in the kitchen and with general housework, I shall often be compelled to call upon you, or rather," she added with a slight caress, "to accept the assistance you are only too ready to give."

"It is too bad," cried the girl, "that Viny doesn't earn her salt! I wonder how you can have patience with her, mother. If I were her mistress, I'd have sent her off at a moment's warning long before this."

"Let us try to imitate God's patience with us, which is infinite," Mrs. Keith answered low and reverently. "Let us bear with her a little longer. But indeed, I do not know that we could fill her place with anyone who would be more competent or satisfactory in any way."

"I'm afraid that is quite true, but it does seem hard that such a woman as my gifted, intellectual, and accomplished mother should have to spend her life in the drudgery of housework, cooking, mending, and taking care of babies."

"No, dear. You are taking the wrong view of it. God appoints our lot. He chooses all our changes for us. Jesus, the God-man, dignified manual labor by making it his own employment during a great part of His life on earth, and 'it is enough for the disciple that he be as his Master, and the servant as his Lord.'

"Besides, what sweeter work can a mother have than the care and training of her own offspring?"

"But then what of the cooking, mother, and all the rest of it?"

"Well, dear, the health, and consequently the happiness and usefulness of my husband and children, depend very largely upon the proper preparation of their food. So that is no mean task."

"Ah, mother, you are determined to make a good case and not to believe yourself poorly used," said Mildred, smiling, yet speaking in a half-petulant tone.

"No, I am not poorly used. My life is crowned with mercies, of the very least of which I am utterly unworthy," her mother answered gently.

"And, my child, I find that any work is sweet when done 'heartily as to the Lord and not unto men!' What is sweeter than a service of love! 'Be ye followers of God as dear children.'"

"Yes," said Aunt Wealthy, coming in at the moment. "'as dear children,' not as servants or slaves, but doing the will of God from the heart. Not that we may be saved, but because we are saved. Our obedience is not the ground of our acceptance but the proof of our love to Him and our faith in Him who freely gives us the redemption purchased by His own blood. Oh what a blessing it is! How sweet to belong to Jesus and to owe everything to Him!"

"I feel so," Mrs. Keith said with an undertone of deep joy in her sweet voice.

"And I," whispered Mildred, laying her head in her mother's lap as she knelt at her side, as had been her wont in childish days.

They were all silent after that for many minutes, sitting there in the gloaming, Mrs. Keith's hand passing softly, caressingly over her daughter's hair and cheeks. Then Mildred spoke.

"Let me try it, mother dear, teaching the children, I mean. You know there is nothing that helps one more to be thorough, and I want to fit myself for teaching if ever I should have my own living to earn."

"Well, well, my child, you may try."

"That's my own dear mother!" exclaimed the girl joyfully, starting up to catch and kiss the hand that had been caressing her. "Now, I must arrange my plans. I shall have to be very systematic in order to do all I wish."

"Yes," said Miss Stanhope, "one can accomplish very little without a system but often a great deal with one."

Mildred set to work with cheerfulness and a great deal of energy and determination and showed herself not easily conquered by difficulties. The rest of that week was given to planning and preparing for her work. On the following Monday, her long-neglected studies were resumed and her duties as family governess entered into.

These took up the morning from nine to twelve, but by early rising and diligence, she was able to do a great deal about the house before the hour for lessons to begin.

Her mother insisted that she must have an hour of recreation every afternoon, taking a walk when weather permitted, then another for study, and the two with Mr. Lord left but a small margin for anything else. Sewing and reading with mother and sisters usually filled out the remainder of the day.

Sometimes her plans worked well, and she was able to go through the round of self-imposed duties with satisfaction to herself and to that of her mother and aunt, who looked on with great interest and were ever on the watch to lend a helping hand and keep hindrances out of her way.

But these last would come now and again in the shape of callers, accidents, or mischievous pranks on the part of the little ones or delinquencies on that of the maid until at times Mildred's patience and determination were sorely tried.

She would grow discouraged and be nearly ready to give up, then summon all her energies to the task, battle with her difficulties, and for a time rise superior to them.

But a new foe appeared upon the field and vanquished her. It was the ague, attacking now one and now another of the family. Soon they were seldom all well, and it was no uncommon thing for two or three to be down with it at once. Viny took it and left, and they hardly knew whether to be glad or sorry.

Governessing had to be given up, nursing and housework substituted for that and for sewing and reading. For some weeks longer, the lessons with Mr. Lord were kept up, but at length they also had to be dropped, for Mildred herself succumbed to the malaria and grew too weak, ill, and depressed for study.

# Chapter Twelfth

*We're not ourselves*
*When nature, being oppress'd,*
*commands the mind*
*To suffer with the body.*

—Shakespeare's *King Lear*

THE NEIGHBORS WERE very kind, coming in with offers of assistance in nursing the sick, bringing dainties to tempt their appetites, encouraging them with the assurance that they were but sharing the common lot. Almost everybody expected a chill about once in two or three weeks, especially this time of the year, and they weren't often disappointed. They thought themselves fortunate if they could stop at one paroxysm till the week came round again.

Quinine would generally stop it, and when people had a long siege of the ague, they often got used to it so far as to manage to keep up and about their work—if not at all times, at least between chills, which as a general thing came only every other day.

Indeed, it was no unusual thing for them to feel quite bright and well on the intermediate day.

The Lightcaps were not a whit behind the others in these little acts of kindness. Rhoda Jane forgot her envy of Mildred on learning that she was sick and seemed to have lost her relish for food.

One morning Miss Stanhope, who was getting breakfast, was favored with an early call from Miss Lightcap.

She appeared at the open kitchen door, basket in hand, and marched in without stopping to knock. "I heerd Miss Mildred was sick and couldn't eat nothin'," she said. "I knowed you hadn't no garden sass o' your own. So I fetched over some tomats. We have a lot this year, real splendid big ones, and there ain't nothin' tastes better when you're gettin' over the agur, than tomats.

"Just you cut 'em up with vinegar and pepper and salt, and if she don't say they're first-rate eatin'—I'm mistaken. That's all."

"Thank you. You're very kind, Miss Nightcap," said Aunt Wealthy, looking so pleased and grateful that the girl could not take the misnomer as an intentional insult.

"P'shaw!" she said. "It's nothin'. We've plenty of 'em."

Having emptied her basket upon the table, she was starting for the door but looked back.

"Say, do you want a girl?"

"Yes, indeed, if we can get one that's worth anything."

"Well, Celestia Ann Hunsinger told me that she wouldn't mind coming here for a spell. 'Cause she wants money to git new clo'es."

"What sort of girl is she?"

"She's pretty high-strung and spunky, but she's punkuns for hard work."

"Thank you. I'll tell Mrs. Keith about it and send you word directly after breakfast."

"All right. I guess she'll come if you want her."

Rhoda Jane had just gone when the door at the foot of the stairs opened and Mildred's pale face appeared.

"Aunt Wealthy, it is too bad to see you at work here. Let me get breakfast. I do think I can. The children are dressing each other; mother has the baby and won't let me do anything up there."

"Well, you'll not find me a whit more tractable," returned Miss Stanhope. "Let you get breakfast, indeed! I'd be worse than a brute if I did.

"Go into the sitting room and lie down on the lounge," she continued, taking up one of the finest tomatoes and beginning to divest it of its skin. "I'll bring you something presently that I really hope will taste good to you.

"That Miss Heavycap brought you a present. She's not over-refined, but she's good-hearted, I think, in spite of her rude ways and rough talk."

"Yes, they have been very kind and neighborly. I wish they were the sort of people one could enjoy being intimate with," Mildred said languidly. "Auntie, let me skin those tomatoes."

"Child, you look ready to drop."

"Do I?" she asked, smiling faintly. "Well, I'll sit down to do it. I really can't let you do everything. How fine and large these are. Are they what Rhoda Jane brought over?"

"Yes, for your breakfast. I hope you'll relish them and the cornpone I have in the oven, too."

"See here! Haven't I learned how?" cried Rupert exultingly, stepping in at the open door and holding up a foaming bucket of milk. "Viny never persuaded old Suky to give us so much."

"It's beautiful," said Aunt Wealthy, taking it from him with a congratulatory smile. "I'll strain it at once before the cream begins to rise."

"I'll carry the pans down cellar. What more can I do, auntie?"

"You may draw the butter up out of the well, presently, when breakfast is quite ready."

"And I'll let it down again when the meal's over. Hello, Milly! Is that you? How white and weak you look!"

"Yes," she said, laying the last tomato in the dish. "I believe I'll have to lie down, as Aunt Wealthy bade me, till breakfast is ready."

She tottered into the sitting room and laid herself down on the lounge, feeling so miserably weak and forlorn and so homesick for the old home where they had all enjoyed good health that the tears would come in spite of every effort to restrain them.

Breakfast was to be eaten here. The table was already set—neatly, too—with snowy cloth, shining silver, and delicate china. But there was a look of discomfort about the room that vexed and tried her orderly soul—sand on the carpet, dust on the furniture, children's toys, and a few articles of clothing scattered here and there—and she had no strength to rise and put it in order.

"And no one else is much better able," she sighed to herself, "for Aunt Wealthy, mother, and Zillah have all had chills within a week. Oh, dear, this dreadful country! Why did we ever come to it?"

She heard her father's voice in the kitchen.

"Here, Aunt Wealthy, is some steak. It's better than usual, I think. Can we have a bit broiled for breakfast?"

Miss Stanhope's cheery tones came in reply, "Yes, Stuart, I'll put it right on. I'm so glad you succeeded in getting some fresh meat. It's something of a rarity to us in these days, and I hope they'll all relish it, Marcia and Milly, especially, for they both need something to build up their strength."

"Where are they? Not able to be up?"

His tone was anxious and concerned.

Mildred did not catch the words of Miss Stanhope's reply, but the door opened and her father came to her side, stooped over her, and kissed her pale cheek tenderly.

"How are you, daughter? Don't be discouraged. We'll have you all right before long."

"Oh, father, I'm so out of heart," she sobbed, raising herself to put her arms around his neck and lay her head on his shoulder.

"Oh, that won't do! You must be brave and hopeful," he said, stroking her hair. "You're not so very ill, my child. Ague is not a dangerous disease."

"It isn't that, but there's so much to be done and nobody to do it. We're all so poorly."

"Don't fret about the work. We'll find someone to do it."

"But they don't do it right. Viny never would make up a bed straight or sweep or dust without leaving half the dirt behind her. And when she washed, she faded the calicoes, shrank the flannels, and made the white clothes a wretched color—and she tore them to pieces with hard rubbing and wringing."

"Well, we'll have to just try not to mind these trifles or be too particular," he said soothingly. "Ah, here comes the breakfast," he said as Miss Stanhope, Rupert, Zillah, and Ada trooped in, each bearing a dish. "Let me help you to the table."

"I don't feel in the least hungry," she objected.

"Then eat to please your father."

"And mother, too," said Mrs. Keith coming in with Baby Annis in her arms. "Come, daughter dear, auntie has prepared an excellent meal for us with some help from our kind neighbors, too, I hear."

"Yes," assented Miss Stanhope, "and I've directed them according to preparations, and they do taste good. Come now. When I see you eating, I'll tell you a bit of news the girl brought besides."

Mildred laughed, felt her spirits begin to rise, tasted the tomatoes, pronounced them excellent, and went on to make a good, hearty meal.

The world looked brighter after that.

It had been decided to try Miss Hunsinger if she would come. Mr. Keith went in search of her shortly after breakfast, and within an hour she was duly installed into office.

She was a tall, strong woman with rather a large proportion of bone and muscle—ditto of self-conceit and impudence united to uncommon energy and decision. She held a tremendous faculty of turning out a great amount of work, doing it thoroughly well, too.

At first, she seemed a great improvement upon Viny, and Mildred's heart rejoiced in a complete sweeping, dusting, and setting to rights of the whole house.

The children had been sent out to play in the shade of the sapling grove, while Mrs. Keith supervised the operations of the new help and Miss Stanhope and Mildred busied themselves in the parlor—the one with the week's mending for the family, the other over her neglected studies.

"She's a real new broom, is my Celestia Ann," said Mrs. Keith, coming cheerily in, "leaving no dirty corners or cobwebs and no wrinkles whatever in sheets or spreads."

"Oh, mother, what a blessing!" cried Mildred. "If she'll only stay so."

"Ah, there's the rub! She cannot be a rose without a thorn. What was it Rhoda Jane said of her, Aunt Wealthy?"

The lady reflected a moment before she answered.

"'Punkuns,' large potatoes, I think it was, Marcia, which I understood to mean that she was a good worker. Something also that gave me the impression that she might be high-tempered and saucy. But as you say, we cannot expect thorns without roses."

"She's getting dinner now," remarked Mrs. Keith, "and seems to feel as much at home there as about her other work. I've told her what to get and showed her where everything is, and now I shall leave her to her own devices and see what will be the result."

Half an hour later, the door of the parlor, where now the whole family gathered, was thrown open with the announcement,

"Dinner's ready—all on the table here."

Having made the summons, Miss Hunsinger rushed back to the table in advance of the family, seated herself, spread out her elbows upon it, and with a nonchalant air said, "Come, folks, it's all ready. Set right up."

There was a rapid exchange of glances among the party addressed, but not a word of remonstrance or disapproval was uttered. Physically unequal to the work that must be done, they were helpless in the hands of their help.

The meal was begun in a profound silence that she was the first to break.

"Ther's some hot biscuits out thar," she said with a jerk of her head toward the kitchen door.

"You may bring some in," said Mrs. Keith.

"Just let one o' your gals do it this time; I will next. Turnabout's fair play, you know."

Mildred's eyes flashed, and she opened her lips to speak. But she closed them firmly as she thought of the consequences to her mother and aunt should this girl be sent away before she was able to take up even a part of the burden of the work.

"I'll go, mother," said Zillah, hastily leaving her place. "I don't mind it, but if I were paid for doing it, I would want to earn my money by doing it myself."

"Well, my dear, what do you think of your new help?" queried Mr. Keith, mischievously, when they had withdrawn to the privacy of the parlor.

"The thorn is rather large and sharp," she answered laughingly, "but we are not the only people in the world who must make a choice of evils."

"For my part," Mildred said severely, "I think it's a species of dishonesty to take pay for doing the work of a family and then ask them to do it themselves."

"Aren't you a trifle too hard on her, dear?" asked Miss Stanhope. "It was forward and impertinent, maybe, but I think hardly dishonest. She is not expected to do all the work of the family."

"Here comes Emmaretta Lightcap," said Ada, who was standing in the open doorway. "She has on a faded calico dress, a sunbonnet, and she has bare feet, just as usual. She has a tin pan in her hands."

"Come in, Emmaretta."

The girl stepped over the threshold and approaching Mrs. Keith said, "Here's more tomats mother sent you and a bird for her," pointing to Mildred. "Goto—he's been out shootin', and he sent it to her."

"He's very kind. Take him my thanks for it," said Mildred, coloring, and vexed with herself for doing so. "Please tell your sister, too, that I thank her for the tomatoes and that I liked them very much."

"Are you a-comin' to our school? Miss Damaris she said you was," said the child, turning to Ada while waiting for her pan, which Zillah had carried away to empty.

"No! No, indeed!" cried Ada. "I don't think I like her, and I wouldn't go there for anything!"

"Hush, Ada! You don't know Miss Drybread," said Mrs. Keith, quite surprised at the outbreak.

"Yes, mother. Don't you remember she was here one day?"

"Rhoda Jane, she's comin' over to see you this evenin'," said the little maid, taking her pan and departing as quickly as she came.

Mildred's countenance fell. She appreciated Rhoda Jane's kindness, but she could not enjoy her society.

"Why, Ada," said Mr. Keith, "I knew nothing of your dislike for Miss Drybread. So, when she met me in the street this morning and asked me to send her a scholar, I thought of Milly's sickness and that she must not have so much to do. I promised her that you should go."

"Oh, father!" exclaimed the child, beginning to cry.

Then they all tried to comfort her, and finally she grew in a measure reconciled to her fate.

# CHAPTER THIRTEENTH

*'Tis with our judgments as our watches, none
Go just alike, yet each believes his own.*

—POPE

"YOU HAIN'T RETURNED more'n our fust call, and then you didn't stay but ten minutes," Rhoda Jane said in a half-offended tone to Mildred. "And we're such near neighbors, too. We'd ought to be real sociable."

Mildred apologized by stating the fact that her time was very fully occupied.

"Well, you and Claudina Chetwood seems to be pretty thick. But the Chetwoods is richer'n we are, an I s'pose that makes it easier to find time to visit with 'em."

"The riches don't make any difference," said Mildred, flushing. "And I have heard that the Chetwoods are not very rich."

"Well, they hold their heads high anyway.

"I'm agoin' to have a rag carpet party pretty soon and give you an invite, and if you don't come, I'll be so mad I won't never come near you again."

"Perhaps I will be sick with the ague," sighed Mildred, hoping in her secret heart that it might turn out so.

"Oh, then, of course, I couldn't be mad. But I'll try to have it when you're well."

"When is it to be? And what is it like?"

"Soon's mother and me gits the rags all cut—'bout a week from now, I reckon. Why, a passel o' girls gits together and sews the rags and winds 'em up into balls, and after a while, the boys come in, and then we have lots o' fun and good things to eat. Now I must run home. Good-bye. Mind, you're to be sure to come."

This was Friday. On the ensuing Monday morning, little Ada set out sorrowfully for Miss Drybread's school in company with Emmaretta and Minerva Lightcap.

Mildred was alone in the parlor when the child came back at noon.

"Well, kitten, how was it?" she asked with a sympathetic smile.

"It was awful! Oh, Mildred, she isn't a lady or a Christian, for she deceives and she acts lies. She made a naughty girl believe she was going to roast her to death. There's a stove and big oven in it, and she said she was going to put her in there and build up a hot fire and cook her."

"Did the little girl believe it?"

"Yes. She was dreadfully frightened, and she screamed like everything and promised that indeed, and indeed, she'd be good. Then, Miss Drybread let her go to her seat."

"That was acting a lie and telling one, too, and anybody who would do so is unfit to have the care of children," said Mildred. "I shall tell father and mother about it today, and I'm very sure they won't send you any longer than this one quarter anyhow."

"Mildred, she doesn't look like a lady, either. She doesn't wear anything white round her neck, just a pink calico cape and an apron of the same and another kind of calico dress."

"No matter about that if she only acted and talked right. She's neat and clean, I suppose?"

"Yes. I didn't see any soil on her clothes."

"Well, learn your lessons well and behave nicely, so that she can't find any excuse for ill-treating you."

Mildred looked upon the expected rag carpet party with nearly as great aversion as Ada felt for her new school, but she was a good deal relieved by learning from Claudina Chetwood that she, too, had been notified of its approach and was expected to attend.

"I didn't know that you visited the Lightcaps," said Mildred.

"Oh, yes. They are not cultivated people or very refined. But they're clever folks and kind neighbors, especially in times of sickness, and they would feel dreadfully hurt if one should decline their invitations. They're not the sort of people we exchange formal calls with; indeed, they never make them. But, as mother says, while society here is in the crude state it is now, it will not do to insist upon making associates of only those who are congenial."

"Or quite belong to our station?"

"Yes. We cannot divide up into many circles and must be willing to mix to some extent with all who can lay claim to respectability and moral worth."

"I'm afraid I'm very proud," said Mildred, vividly blushing. "I've never been used to associating with anyone so rough and uncouth, and it goes a good deal against the grain."

"Perhaps it isn't exactly pride," suggest Claudina. "They offend your taste—they do mine, I know—but surely we can bear that rather than give them the pain of thinking that we don't like them."

"Yes, indeed," assented Mildred heartily, and from that moment, she ceased to allow herself to hope that something would occur to give her a plausible excuse for staying away from Rhoda Jane's merrymaking.

She repeated Claudina's remarks to her mother and aunt and found that they fully approved of the sentiments she had expressed.

"There was a time when I should have been very unwilling to see you consort with that class," said Mrs. Keith, "but circumstances alter cases."

The invitation came for Friday afternoon and evening, Rhoda Jane hailing Rupert as he passed and sending it through him.

Mildred was nearly in her usual health and accepted without a demur. But she was puzzled about what to wear and at what hour to go, and so went to Claudina for instruction on these important points.

"We are invited to work, you know," said Miss Chetwood, laughing, "so, we will be expected early. We should not be later than one o'clock, I think, and as it is not very nice work—carpet rags being apt to be dusty—we should not wear anything that will not wash. I shall put on a calico dress and carry a big work apron with me."

"Then I shall do the same."

"I wish you would, for there will be some girls there who haven't the means to dress and would feel badly if you or I outshone them very much."

"I can't go before three or half-past, though, on account of having to recite to Mr. Lord."

"Never mind. I daresay it's just as well, for you'll get quite enough of both the work and the company."

Following the instructions received, Mildred attired herself for the occasion with the utmost simplicity. But she could not lay aside her delicate prettiness or a certain air of culture and refinement that made her more the real lady in her calico than almost any of her companions of the afternoon would have been in the richest silk or velvet.

Just as she was ready to go, Ada came in from school, crying heartily.

"What's the matter?" asked Mildred, meeting her on the threshold and turning back full of sympathy.

"I—I've lost my place in the spelling class," sobbed the child, "and I didn't miss a word, either. You know I got up to the head the first day, and I've kept there ever since—'way above all those big, big girls—some of 'em as big as you, Milly."

"But how did you get down, if you didn't miss? Was it for bad behavior?"

"No, but she upset the class and made us all draw lots for our places. The one I drew made my place next to the foot."

"Mother, do you hear that?" asked Mildred hotly, for anything like abuse or unjust treatment of her little brothers and sisters was sure to rouse her ire.

"Yes," Mrs. Keith said, "but Ada, you like the fun of moving up in your class. You could never have that if you were always at the head."

This seemed a new idea to the child, and she smiled faintly through her tears.

But the wound was so deep it must bleed awhile, and the briny drops fell fast again.

She was an uncommonly good speller for a child of her age, and she had taken great pride in keeping her place, working very hard to be able to do so. This sudden, unexpected downfall, due to no failure on her part, almost overwhelmed her with a sense of loss, humiliation, and injustice.

Mildred waited. She couldn't bear to go and leave Ada in such distress.

"Don't cry," she said, stroking Ada's hair caressingly, while the mother wiped away the fast-flowing tears with her own soft, white handkerchief and kissed the flushed cheek. "Don't cry. You'll soon get up again."

"And I shall write a note to Miss Drybread, telling her that I cannot approve of drawing lots to decide so trivial a matter," said Mrs. Keith. "It seems to me very wrong, because it is an appeal to God. 'The lot is cast into the lap; but the whole disposing thereof is of the Lord.' It might be well enough to turn the class around occasionally, or in some other way to give the poor scholars a chance to rise. But this proceeding I so highly disapprove of that I shall not allow you to take part in it again."

"I wish you'd take me out of her school, mother, oh. please do," pleaded the little girl.

"You shall not be kept there long," Mrs. Keith said. "But Mildred, child," she added merrily, "you must hurry away, or I fear you'll not earn your supper."

A dozen maidens, mostly under twenty years of age, were collected in "the front room" at Mr. Lightcap's. A large clothesbasket filled with many colored rags that had been torn or cut into strips of various lengths occupied a conspicuous place upon the floor.

A number of girls were grouped about it, and armed with needles, thread, scissors, and thimbles, were busily engaged picking out the strips, sewing the ends together, and winding the long strings thus formed into balls. Others had filled their laps and seated themselves here and there about the room.

They seemed a very merry company, laughing and chatting as they worked.

"Oh, how d'ye do?" said Rhoda Jane, catching sight of Mildred as she drew near the door, which was standing open. "Thought you wasn't comin' at all. Walk right in. Let me take your sunbonnet. Here's a seat for you 'long side of Miss Chetwood. Guess you're better acquainted with her than anybody else, unless it's Viny Apple.

"Ladies, this is Miss Keith."

"I don't need no hintroduction," laughed Miss Apple. "'Ope you're well, Miss Milly."

The others looked up with a nod and a murmured word or two, as Rhoda Jane named each in turn. They seemed to take up the thread of their discourse where it had been dropped, while Mildred tied on her apron, took the chair assigned her, threaded a needle, and helping herself, by invitation, from Claudina's lap, began her first ball, at the same time explaining that her lessons had detained her.

"You must be goin' to be dreadful learned," commented Rhoda Jane, filling Mildred's lap from the basket, "I wouldn't be you for anything. I hate books and always did."

"Are we all here now?" asked someone.

"All but Damaris Drybread. She's oldish for the rest of us, but she's the schoolma'am, you know, and likes to be invited. And though she's late comin'— yonder she is now—she works dreadful fast when she does get at it."

Mildred overheard a whisper not complimentary to the coming woman, "P'shaw! I wish she hadn't been asked. She spoils everything, for she's as solemn as a funeral and 'pears to think it's a sin to laugh."

"Yes," assented another voice, "that's so! And she never forgets that she's a schoolma'am but takes it upon herself to tell you your duty without waiting to be invited to."

But now Miss Drybread was upon the threshold.

"Good evening," she said in solemn tone and with a stiff little bow, addressing her salutation to the company in general. Then, giving her sunbonnet to

Rhoda Jane, she seated herself in her usual bolt upright manner and fell to work.

Her presence acted as a damper upon the spirits of the younger portion of the party. A dead silence succeeded the merry chatter and laughter of a moment before.

Mildred had cared little for that while it went on, but it vexed her now that this woman, for whom, principally on Ada's account, she began to feel a decided dislike, should have it in her power thus to spoil the enjoyment of others. Thus, she determined that it should not be so.

Raising her voice that all might hear, she told an amusing anecdote that set everybody to laughing except the schoolma'am, whose increasing solemnity of aspect seemed to reprove their levity.

"Oh, that was first rate! Do tell us another," cried Rhoda Jane, holding her sides. "I had no idea you could be so funny."

Mildred went on with anecdotes, puns, jests, conundrums, Claudina and one or two others contributing their quota also, until, with the ruder ones, the mirth became somewhat boisterous. As it died down again, Miss Drybread spoke.

"Life, permit me to observe to you all, is too serious and solemn to be spent in laughing and joking. Allow me to say, Miss Keith, that I am astonished that you, a church member, should indulge in such frivolity."

"Do you think a Christian should always wear a long face, ma'am?" asked Mildred saucily, her tell-tale countenance showing all too plainly the contempt and obvious aversion she felt for her self-constituted censor.

"Yes. I think that folks that profess that they've got religion ought to be grave and sober and let the world see that they don't belong to it."

"As if there was any harm in innocent mirth!" exclaimed Mildred. "As if there was anybody in the world with so good a right to be glad and happy as one who knows that Jesus loves him! 'Rejoice in the Lord, ye righteous and shout for joy all ye that are upright in heart.' The Bible is full of commands for God's people to rejoice, to be glad, to sing for joy, and the best Christians I know seem to me the happiest people on earth."

"You're rather young to set up your judgment as to who's the best Christian and who's got religion and who hasn't," returned the spinster, bridling.

"Well, none o' your long-faced, sour-looking Christians for me!" exclaimed Rhoda Jane. "I'd never want to get religion till the last minute if I wasn't to be 'lowed to laugh and joke no more."

"I cannot read the heart, nor can any other human creature," said Mildred, replying to Miss Drybread's last remark. "But Jesus says, 'By their fruits ye shall know them,' and 'He that keepeth my commandments, he it is that loveth me.' When you live with people and see them constantly serving God with gladness, walking in His ways, rejoicing in His love, making the Bible always their rule of faith and practice, showing far more solicitude about heavenly than about earthly things, both for themselves and their children, I think you may be very sure they are real Christians."

"I think so, too!" said Claudina emphatically.

"So do I," "and I," chimed in several other voices. "But do you know any such folks?"

"I have been describing my father and mother," Mildred said. "And my dear Aunt Wealthy, too."

"That's a fact," spoke up Viny. "You 'ave to live with folks to find 'em out, and I've lived there, and I never seen better Christians. They don't keep their religion for Sundays, but Mr. Keith, 'e reads in the Good Book hevery night and mornin' and prays just like a minister—honly not so long—and they sing 'ymns. And I never 'eard a cross word pass between Mr. and Mrs. Keith—or Miss Stan'ope heither, and they never threaten the children they'll do something hawful like breakin' their bones or skinnin' 'em alive, has some folks does. They just speaks to 'em quiet like, sayin' exactly what they mean, and they're always minded, too."

# Chapter Fourteenth

*Jest and youthful jollity,*
*Quips and cranks and wanton wiles,*
*Nods and becks and wreathed smiles.*

"THERE HAD BETTER be less talk, if these are all to be sewed today," remarked Miss Drybread, taking a fresh supply from the basket and straightening herself till she was, if possible, more erect than before.

"I can talk and work, too. My needle hain't stopped because my tongue was runnin'," retorted Viny. "It strikes me you've been doin' your share as well's the rest."

"There, this ball's all done," said Claudina, tossing it up in the air.

"It's a good, big one, too, and wound real tight," said Rhoda Jane, taking it, giving it a squeeze, then rolling in into a corner where quite a pile had collected.

"How quick you are, Claudina," said Mildred.

"Not so very. I've been at it quite a good while. Some folks can pretty nearly make two to my one." She glanced toward Miss Drybread who was just beginning to wind her second.

"But 'tain't everybody that winds 'em as good and solid as you do, Claudina," said another girl significantly. "Windin' loose can make a ball grow fast, I tell you!"

"'All is not gold that glitters,'" quoted Mildred.

"I'd begin to wind, if I were you," said Claudina. "You have quite a pile there, Mildred, and it might get into a tangle."

"Thank you. I'm new at this business," said Mildred, laughing. "I shall take the advice of an older hand."

"Supper's ready," announced Minerva, opening the kitchen door.

"Put down your rags and walk right out, ladies," said Rhoda Jane.

"It seems to me that I, for one, need some preparation," said Mildred, dropping hers and looking at her hands.

"Oh, yes, we'll wash out here," said Rhoda Jane, leading the way.

A tin bucket full of water, a dipper, and washbasin, all bright from a recent scouring, stood on a bench in the shed at the outer kitchen door. A piece of brown soap lay there also, and a clean towel hung on a nail in the wall close by.

The girls used these in turn, laughing and chatting merrily all the while. Then they gathered about the table, which was bountifully spread with good country fare—chicken, ham, dried beef, pickles, tomatoes, cucumbers, radishes, cheese, eggs, pie, cakes, and preserves in several varieties. There were also hot cakes and cold bread, tea and coffee.

None of the family partook with their guests except Rhoda Jane. They would eat afterward, and Mrs. Lightcap busied herself now in waiting upon the table, filling the tea and coffee cups in the shed where the cooking stove stood during the months of the year when its heat was objectionable in the house.

"I don't know as we've earned our supper, Mis' Lightcap," remarked one of the girls, stirring her tea. "We hain't begun to git all them rags sewed up yet."

"Well, then, I'll just set you to work again as soon as you're done eatin'. That'll do just as well; folks don't always pay in advance, you know."

"And if we don't get through 'fore the boys come, we'll make them help," said Rhoda Jane.

"What boys?" queried Mildred, whereat several of the girls giggled.

"Why the fellows, of course," laughed Miss Lightcap. "The boys is what we mostly call 'em, though some of 'em's pretty old, I should judge, for to be called that."

"Yes, there's Rocap Stubblefield. He must be thirty at least," said one.

"And Nick Ransquattle's twenty-five if he's a day," remarked another.

"Well, the rest's young enough," said Mrs. Lightcap. "Pass that cake there, Rhoda Jane. There's my Gotobed, who just turned twenty-one, and Yorke

Mocker, Wallace Ormsby, and Claudina's brother Will's all younger by some months or a year or so."

The meal concluded, the work went on quite briskly again, Mildred catching now and then a whispered word or two about the desirableness of getting through with it in time to have some fun. But the raw material for sewing more balls still remained in the basket when "the boys" began to arrive.

Gotobed was naturally among the first. He was quite "slicked up," as Rhoda Jane elegantly expressed it, though his preparations had been made under some difficulties.

The only legitimate way of reaching the second story and his Sunday clothes was by a stairway leading up from the front room, where the girls were.

The windows of his bedroom, however, looked out upon the lean-to that formed the kitchen part of the building and whose roof was not many feet higher than that of the shed.

Watching his opportunity for doing so unseen, he climbed upon the shed, gained the roof of the lean-to, and entered his room by the window.

There was nothing of the dandy about the honest fellow, yet somehow dressing was a slow business with him tonight. He stood before a little square of looking glass hanging on the wall, tying and retying his cravat until it was too dark to see. Then giving up in sheer despair, he went over the roof as he had come and sought his mother, who, with the help of Emmaretta and Minerva, was washing dishes in the kitchen.

"My land!" she exclaimed, as he came in, "what a time you've been up there. I never knowed you to take half so long to dress afore."

"My fingers are all thumbs," he said, a hot flush spreading over his sunburnt face. "I can't tie this decent nohow at all."

"Well, just wait till I can wipe my hands, and I'll do it. There, that'll do. The girls ain't agoin' to look partickler hard at that bit o' black ribbing."

"Maybe not, but I'm obleeged to you all the same for fixin' it right. Is it time to go in?"

"Of course, if you want to."

He passed out the back door and through the yard into the street. He was bashful and did not like to face such a bevy of girls alone, and at the thought of addressing one of their number in particular— Mildred Keith—he felt himself grow hot and uncomfortable. He had been admiring her from a distance all these weeks but had never met her. Much as he desired an acquaintance, his courage seemed hardly equal to seeking it out.

How rough and boorish, how awkward and ill-bred he thought he would certainly appear to one so delicate and refined.

He waited about a little till joined by a fellow mechanic, Nicholas Ransquattle, and they went in to the front room together.

This was a wiser step than Gotobed knew; for his well-made stalwart figure showed to good advantage beside that of Nicholas, who was short and thick-set, had scarcely any neck, moved like a wooden man, and carried his head thrown back on his shoulders. He had a wooden face, too—large-featured and stolid in expression.

But he was not troubled with bashfulness or any fear that his society would be other than most acceptable to anyone upon whom he might see fit to bestow it.

"Good evening, ladies. I'm happy to meet you all," he said, making a sweeping bow to the company as he entered with hat in hand. "I hope I find you well."

"Good evening," responded several voices. "Good evening, Mr. Lightcap."

"Find yourselves seats, and we'll give you some employment, threading our needles for us."

Rhoda Jane was snuffing the candles. Hastily laying down her snuffers, she introduced the young men to Mildred and dexterously managed to seat Ransquattle on the farther side of the room, leaving the field clear for her brother, for an empty chair stood invitingly at Miss Keith's side.

Gotobed took it and, almost wondering at his own audacity, addressed her with a remark upon the weather—that never-failing source when all other topics elude us.

She answered with gracious sweetness, "Yes, it has been a lovely day, Mr. Lightcap."

What should he say next?

"I—I guess you never sewed carpet rags afore?"

"Is it my awkwardness at the business that makes you think so?" she returned with a quizzical look and smile as she lifted her fine eyes to his face.

"No, no, no siree, er, ma'am, I mean," he stammered, growing red and hot. "You do it beautiful!"

"Let me give you some work," she said, taking pity on his embarrassment. "Will you thread this needle for me?"

"And then mine, also, please," put in Claudina, who was again seated near her friend. To his further relief, she launched into a pleasant reminiscence of a candy pulling they had both attended the year before.

Others of "the boys" came flocking in, the work was speedily finished, and there was some tossing back and forth of the balls amid rather uproarious laughter. But some of them unwound and became entangled, and so that sport was given up. The girls washed their hands as before supper, and Blindman's Buff, Kitten in the Corner, and other games were played with as much zest as if the players had been a parcel of children. Refreshments followed and were served up in the kitchen. There were huckleberries with cream and sugar, watermelons, muskmelons, doughnuts, and cupcakes.

At eleven o'clock, the party broke up, and the young men saw the girls safely home, Gotobed being so fortunate as to secure the privilege of walking Mildred to her father's door.

She would, perhaps, have slightly preferred the attentions of Yorke Mocker or Wallace Ormsby, both of whom she had met before and who were young men of much better education and much more polish and refinement than poor Gotobed.

It was Mrs. Keith who admitted her daughter, everyone else in the house having retired.

"Had you a pleasant time?" she asked with a motherly smile.

"I heard some of the others, as they went away, saying it had been perfectly splendid," Mildred answered with an amused little laugh. "But the fun was rather too rough of a sort for me."

"Games?"

"Yes, ma'am, and I took part until they began kissing, then I retired to the ranks of the spectators."

"That was right," Mrs. Keith said emphatically.

"And what do you think, mother," Mildred laughed, "Viny Apple was one of the guests. The idea of being invited out to meet your former housemaid and cook! Isn't it too funny?"

"Well, dear, let us be thankful that Celestia Ann was not invited also, leaving me to get tea tonight," Mrs. Keith said, joining in the laugh.

# CHAPTER FIFTEENTH

*The knight, perusing this epistle,*
*Believ'd h' had brought her to his whistle.*
*And read it like a jocund lover,*
*With great applause t' himself twice over.*

—BUTLER

RHODA JANE HAD set the ball in motion, and for several weeks similar festivities were much in vogue among the young people of Pleasant Plains. There were other rag carpet bees; some quilting, berrying, and nutting parties; boatings on the river; and buggy rides and rides on horseback.

Then as the days grew short and the evenings long, a singing school was started. It met once a week at Damaris Drybread's schoolroom and was largely attended by the youth of both sexes, quite as much for the sport to be had from it as for the improvement of their vocal powers.

Each carried thither a notebook and a tallow candle, and at the end of the term, each paid his or her portion of the salary of the teacher—one Timothy Buzzard from a neighboring town.

Not the fittest name in the world for a singing teacher, people said, but then he couldn't help that.

He soon proved himself competent for what he had undertaken—for imparting instruction, at least. As to keeping order among his pupils, some of whom were years older than himself, that he found was quite another thing. Of course, there was often a good deal of misbehavior on the part of the silly, giggling girls and tittering lads which tried his patience, occasionally even beyond endurance.

Mildred, Claudina, and their friend Lucilla Grange were not of these, but they invariably conducted themselves in a ladylike manner, which won the admiration and gratitude of the sometimes sorely-tried teacher and gave him a powerful motive to self-control in the natural desire to win their respect and esteem.

The three girls were the belles of the town. Timothy was an unmarried man, and when he seemed to pay court in any manner to one or another of them, several of the young men were inclined to grow wrathy over it and to feel that their rights were thus invaded.

Will Chetwood, Yorke Mocker, and Wallace Ormsby had become frequent visitors at Mr. Keith's, though perhaps not more so in the case of the latter two than at the homes of Mildred's intimate girl friends. The six formed a coterie of their own and were generally seen together at the merry-makings, pairing off now in one way, now in another.

Gotobed Lightcap would now and then pluck up courage to step in upon Mildred on an evening, and he was invariably treated politely and kindly, though not in a way as to give undo encouragement.

He had an instinctive understanding of that, attributed it in a great measure to his own awkward, ungainly ways, and looked with envy upon those whose better education and more polished manners made them more acceptable companions.

Nicholas Ransquattle was not one of that number, yet he esteemed himself such and annoyed Mildred not a little by his unwelcome attentions.

They were declined whenever it could be done without positive rudeness, but vanity and self-conceit are often very blind.

Nicholas was quite a reader for a man of his station and limited opportunities. His family were proud of his attainments — he even more so. He was given to displaying them on all possible occasions, often wasting a great deal of breath in the charitable effort to enlighten the ignorance of his associates.

He would call at Mr. Keith's early in the evening, and if occasion offered, talk to Mildred by the hour of his "abstruse studies" and the lighter literature with which he found it necessary to "unbend his mind from them," till she voted him an intolerable bore. He became the laughing stock of her younger brothers and sisters, who found his clumsy, lumbering movements, self-conceit, and egotistical discourse so mirth-provoking that they learned to be on the lookout for him and to find excuses to remain in the room while he stayed, in which last endeavor they all received every encouragement from Mildred.

Meanwhile, so blinded by egotism was the man that he supposed himself an object of great admiration to them and had little if any doubt that the whole family were ready to receive him with open arms whenever he should choose to make a formal proposal for Mildred's hand.

He was a shoemaker by trade and had a little shop on the principal business street of the town, just opposite the store of Chetwood and Mocker — Claudina's brother and cousin.

Mr. Keith had opened an office next door to them, and Wallace Ormsby was diligently studying law with him.

Nicholas sometimes envied Wallace Ormsby the prospective distinction of being a member of one of the learned professions, and while busied with his waxed ends and awl, he considered the propriety of offering himself to Mr. Keith as both a student and a son-in-law both in one.

He finally decided that the marriage proposal to Mildred should be made first, with the other to follow immediately upon her joyful acceptance.

Winter had come in earnest. The ground had frozen hard, and a heavy fall of snow upon this good foundation had made excellent sleighing. The young folks were jubilant over it, and more than one plan for its enjoyment had been set afloat.

"Mornin', Nick. See here. I want you to make me a pair o' new boots. Put your very best work on 'em," said Gotobed Lightcap, entering Nicholas Ransquattle's shop after a moment's vigorous kicking and hearty stamping of the snow from his feet upon the doorstep.

"All right, Gote. Sit down and off with your boots," returned Nicholas, putting down his awl and taking up his measures.

"Let me have 'em as soon as you can," said Gotobed. "And be sure to make 'em a neat fit," he added, laughing. "Or else, they'll maybe be throwed back on your hands."

"They'll give satisfaction, you may depend," returned Ransquattle, straightening himself and throwing his head back on his shoulders in his accustomed fashion. "Whatever I undertake is always done in the best style."

"Eh! I hadn't noticed," said Gotobed, innocently. "You're goin' sleighing tomorrow night, I s'pose?"

"Yes, and I calculate to take Mildred Keith."

"You do!" Lightcap exclaimed in tones of mingled anger and inquiry, his brows knitting wrathfully and a hot flush dyeing his swarthy cheek. "Have you asked her, got her consent?"

"Her? What her? May I ask?" queried Yorke Mocker, coming in as Gotobed's question was propounded, Wallace Ormsby close at his heels.

"No, I haven't asked her yet, but I shall in the course of the day, "and now I warn you fellows that she's my choice, and you may each pick out some other girl to take to the sleighing."

"Indeed! And may I ask how you came by the right to the first pick?"

"I've as much right to Mildred Keith as anybody else, Mr. Mocker—more, I should say. I'm going to marry her."

There was a simultaneous explosion of astonishment and indignation at his presumption from Mocker and Ormsby, while Lightcap, thinking no one would dare speak with such confident boasting who had not received great encouragement, turned pale, then flushed again as he picked up and drew on the boot he had just taken off.

"I admire the modesty of the man," remarked Wallace Ormsby with cutting sarcasm. "I presume you will find the young lady ready to drop into your arms at the first hint of your intentions."

"Of course, since it must be evident to her that she couldn't possibly do any better," sneered Yorke. "Pray, when did you learn that you were such a favorite?"

"I flatter myself that I do not lack discernment," returned Ransquattle with unmoved self-complaisance, as he entered his measurements in his book, then used his coattail as a pen-wiper. "Anything I can do for you this morning, gentlemen?"

"No," growled Ormsby, "but there's something I can do for you, namely, save you the trouble of asking Miss Keith to go with you tomorrow night by informing you that she has already consented to allow me to be her escort."

"Is that so?" exclaimed Ransquattle, reddening with anger and disappointment. "Well, I must say I think it's very unfair, the way you fellows always get ahead of the rest of us."

"So do I," said Gotobed, leaving the shop and walking away in moody discontent, too much chagrined at learning that he had no chance to even enjoy the discomfiture of Nicholas.

"There has been no unfair dealing about it," retorted Ormsby sharply as he and Mocker followed Gotobed into the street. In their anger and excitement, they had quite forgotten the errand that had brought them to Ransquattle's shop: to borrow his horse and sleigh for the proposed expedition in case he were not going to make use of them himself.

They crossed the street, joined Will Chetwood in the store, and roused his ire also by a recital of what had just occurred.

Ransquattle was angry, too. "No unfair dealing about it, eh!" he muttered, looking after them. "Well, I say there has been. They've managed to keep other fellows at a distance from the girl without any regard to her wishes. But I'll put a stop to that game, my lads. See if I don't."

He took a letter from his pocket as he spoke, unfolded it, handling it tenderly, and glanced over the contents with a smile of self-congratulation.

"Ah, ha! We'll see if she'll be able to resist this!" he said half aloud as he refolded and returned it to its place in the breast pocket of his coat.

A sleigh was at that moment standing at the front door of the yellow house on the corner, and into it Mr. Keith was assisting his wife and aunt. Then followed the babe and the three next in age. They were going to the country to spend the day with their Lansdale acquaintances, the Wards.

Mildred, Rupert, Zillah, and Ada stood in the doorway to see them off. "You won't be back in time for tea?" Mildred asked.

"No, but by bedtime," her father answered as he turned the horses' heads. "Now go in, all of you, out of the cold before you catch the ague."

"What did Claudina say to our invitation?" asked Mildred, addressing Rupert as they obeyed the order.

"Yes, of course. Isn't she always glad of a chance to come here?"

"That's good. How soon?"

"In about half an hour, I believe she said. So you had better hear Ada's lessons and get them out of the way."

It was some weeks now since Ada's heart had been rejoiced by a final deliverance from Miss Drybread's control and a return to the instruction of her sister. Mr. Lord still kept up his class, and Mildred's zeal for study had not abated, but the minister had a funeral to attend at a distant point that afternoon, so there would be no recitation to interfere with the pleasure of the day with Claudina. Celestia Ann still kept her position in the family, and though only ten o'clock, the house was in order, and dinner and tea would require no supervision by the eldest daughter of the house.

Claudina brought her sewing, and the two passed an uneventful but pleasant day together, chatting over their work or reading aloud in turn, for Claudina was nearly as great a lover of books as was Mildred.

Their talk was not largely of their neighbors, but some jests passed between them at Ransquattle's expense. They were quite severe in their criticisms, as young women are too apt to be, but if the ears of the victim burned, it was not enough to prevent the act of folly he still had in contemplation.

Tea was over, and Miss Hunsinger had removed the dishes to the kitchen. Mildred spread a bright-colored cover over the table, placed the candles on it, and she and Claudina settled themselves to their sewing again. Zillah and Ada were the only other occupants of the room, Rupert having gone out.

Presently there came a knock at the outer door.

"I'll go," said Ada, running to open it.

A man, Nicholas Ransquattle, stood on the threshold. Stepping past the child without even speaking, he made directly for Mildred. He silently extended his right hand, between the thumb and forefinger of which he held a letter.

In a sort of daze, the girl took it, and with one of his profound obeisances, of which Cyril had often remarked, "I thought he was going to squattle on the stove when he put his head down so low," Nicholas withdrew without having spoken a word.

They could hear the crackling of the snow under his heavy tread as he walked away.

"Oh, Milly, what is it? What is it? What did he bring it for? Had he been to the post office?" the little girls asked with eager curiosity.

Mildred turned to Claudina. They looked into each other's eyes for a moment and then burst into a simultaneous hearty laugh.

"Did you ever see such a comical performance?"

"Never! It's addressed to you, of course?"

"Yes."

Seizing a candle, laughing and blushing, Mildred said, "Come, help me read it. We'll go upstairs where we won't be disturbed."

"Mayn't we go, too? Mayn't we know what your letter's about?" pleaded the little girls as the older ones hurried away.

"No, no! 'Tisn't the sort for children like you to know about," laughed the sister. "Be good and stay here. We won't be gone long, and someday, perhaps, I'll tell you what it says."

They hurried through the kitchen where Miss Hunsinger was vigorously setting things to rights, up the crooked stairway, and on into Aunt Wealthy's room. They fastened the door and proceeded to examine the missive.

It was an offer to Miss Mildred Keith of the heart, hand, and fortune of the writer, Nicholas Ransquattle, who proclaimed himself her devoted worshipper and slave and addressed her as an angel and the loveliest and sweetest of created beings. The girls giggled over it at first, but at length Mildred threw it down in supreme disgust.

"Such stuff and nonsense! It's perfectly sickening! I'm anything but an angel, especially when I lose my temper. And I believe I'm losing it now, for I feel insulted by an offer from such a conceited fool!"

"Somebody's coming!" exclaimed Claudina.

"Yes. Rupert. I know his step. Well, Ru, what is it?" she said as the boy rapped lightly on the door.

"Before you answer that letter and accept the fellow, let me tell you something."

Mildred threw open the door.

"Who told you I had one?"

"The children told me about old Nick bringing you a letter," he answered, laughing but looking a little angry, too. "It's easy enough to guess the subject, particularly since I heard a bit of news over yonder at the smithy. Gote Lightcap says he heard him—old Nick—boasting this morning, before several young men, that he was going to marry Mildred Keith."

For a minute or more, Mildred did not speak. She had probably never felt so angry in all her life.

"The conceited puppy!" she cried at last. "Wouldn't I like to take some of it out of him!"

"Good for you!" cried Rupert, clapping his hands. "I knew you'd be mad, and wouldn't I just like to horsewhip him for his impudence?"

"But it isn't right," said Mildred, already cooling down a little and ashamed of her outburst. "You couldn't thrash him, Ru, but instead you shall, if you will, have the pleasure of carrying him my answer."

"Tell me what it is first."

Mildred took the letter and wrote in pencil beneath the signature, "The above offer is positively declined; all future visits on the part of the writer also," and signed her name. "There, return it," she said, "with the strict information that it is my final reply."

# Chapter Sixteenth

*Oh jealousy! Thou bane of pleasing friendship,*
*Thou worst invader of our tender bosoms:*
*How does thy rancour poison all our softness,*
*And turn our gentle nature into bitterness!*

—Rowe

The news was too good to keep, and Rupert could not forbear stopping at the smithy on his return and giving Gotobed a hint of how matters stood.

To say that the certainty of a decided rejection of Ransquattle's suit lifted a burden of anxiety from young Lightcap's mind is not an overestimate of the relief that Rupert's communication afforded him.

He had been moody and depressed since his visit of the morning to Ransquattle's shop and had refused to give Rhoda Jane any satisfaction as to his intentions in regard to the sleighing party of the following evening. She was therefore agreeably surprised when toward bedtime he came, in quite a merry mood, into the kitchen where she sat sewing alone, their mother having stepped out to see a neighbor. He had come to tell her that he had decided to go.

"Well, I'm glad of it," she said. "Who are you going to take?"

He colored at the question and answered almost doggedly, "I'm going after Sarah Miller."

"Why don't you ask Mildred Keith?"

"'Cause there ain't no use. Ormsby's headed me off there."

"Yes, an' if you don't look out with yer pokin' ways, he'll head you off altogether, and he'll marry her afore you know it."

"She ain't goin' off in such a hurry," he muttered, drumming on the table with his fingers. Then, jumping up from his chair and going over to the stove, he made a pretense of warming himself so that he might avoid the keen scrutiny of his sister's sharp eyes. "But what's the use o' me a tryin' with all them fellers around?"

"Gote Lightcap, I'm ashamed of you!" exclaimed Rhoda Jane. "If I was a man, I'd have more pluck by a long shot. 'Twouldn't be me that would let any feller get ahead o' where I was a mind to go in and win."

"You don't know nothin' about it," he retorted, lighting a candle and stalking off to bed.

"Dear me, if he only had half my spunk!" said Rhoda Jane, looking after him with scornful eyes and a curling lip.

That very wish was echoed more than once in his heart as he lay awake far into the night revolving the subject in his mind and filled with longings, doubts, and fears.

He had been so greatly rejoiced over the downfall of Ransquattle's hopes, but what did it actually avail him while the other three, whose superiority he could not help acknowledge to himself, remained in the way? Alas, there was no great cause for exultation that one rival out of four had been removed from his path.

Still, was it quite certain that they were all rivals? Might it not be that Miss Chetwood or Miss Grange was the more attractive girl to one or all of them? The six were so constantly seen together, and the attentions of the three young men were so equally divided between the three girls, that who could tell how they were going to pair off, if at all?

Besides, there was no accounting for tastes, and a lady didn't always select that special one from among her admirers or from those whom other people in general considered the most desirable match. There was still a speck of hope for him—ah, if he only had Rhoda Jane's pluck and energy of determination!

Near sunset of the next day, a large omnibus sleigh drawn by four horses with jingling bells and well supplied with buffalo robes and other appliances for keeping the cold at bay went from house to house in Pleasant Plains, picking up the girls and "boys" to the number of a dozen or more. They made a very merry company, as they glided swiftly over the snow for some six to eight miles.

The sleighing was fine, the weather not severe. The moon rose soon after the setting of the sun, and the girls, muffled up in hoods, cloaks, and other wraps, were warm and cozy and vastly enjoyed the ride.

Of course, the lads did the same. They laughed, jested, and sang, and found time flying as swiftly as the horses, who seemed to make nothing of their load.

The destination of the sleighing party was a hotel in a neighboring village, where a supper had been ordered for them some days before. It was served up, hot and savory, shortly after their arrival.

A couple of hours afterward were spent in the parlor of the hotel in social chat and in the playing of games, and here they were joined by Mr. Timothy Buzzard, who taught a singing school in this town also.

"There's another rival," thought Gotobed, quite jealously watching him carry on a lively conversation with Mildred. "'Pears like everybody's after her, and I can't get no chance at all."

Rhoda Jane was equally jealous—partly for her brother but still more for herself because last year Mr. Buzzard had waited upon her more than on any other girl in Pleasant Plains. She considered him her property and, as she put it, "didn't fancy bein' cut out by no newcomer nor by anybody else, for that matter."

Influenced by the desire to separate the two, she was the first to suggest that it was time to start for home. She was agreeably surprised that Mildred promptly seconded the motion.

Some objected, saying there was no hurry, but as it was eleven o'clock, these were overruled by the majority, and the sleigh was presently pronounced ready.

"Can't we make room for another passenger?" someone asked, as amid laughter and jesting, they were crowding into the vehicle.

"Who is it?" queried another.

"Why, Buzzard would—"

"No, we hain't room for no more!" interrupted Gotobed. "We're not agoin' to have the ladies crowded in here."

"Speak fer yerself, Gote Lightcap," spoke up Rhoda Jane with spirit. "There ain't none of us so disobligin' as not to be willin' to scrunch up a little for the sake of accommodatin' a fellow in distress. Set up a little closer, girls, and there'll be lots o' room."

"Yes, the more the merrier, and the closer the warmer," assented Sarah Miller, Gote Lightcap's partner for the expedition, who had noticed with vexation and chagrin his evident interest in Mildred Keith. "Come on, Buzzard," she said, making room for the singing teacher between Rhoda Jane and herself.

"Thank you, ladies. I shall be a thorn between two roses," he said, taking the offered seat with a laugh at his own stale jest.

"Now we've got the singing master along, let's have some music," said Rhoda Jane, when they were fairly on their way.

"Yes, you'll be expected to pay your way, Buzzard," remarked Ormsby.

"I hope I'll always be found willing to do that," he responded. "Miss Lightcap, what shall I sing?"

Highly pleased that the choice was given her, Rhoda Jane promptly named a love song she had heard him sing as a solo.

He gave it, then another selected by Miss Miller, and then turned to Mildred. "I think it is your turn now, Miss Keith," he said.

She proposed a round he had taught them that winter, saying all could join in.

All did so with hearty good will. Other rounds, glees, choruses, and solos followed. They sang even after reaching Pleasant Plains and sang on till but two or three were left as one after another was set down at his or her own door.

A light burned in the parlor at Mr. Keith's, and the front door was opened before the sleigh had quite drawn up to it.

"Poor, dear mother! What a shame to have kept you up so long!" Mildred exclaimed as she came in.

"Never mind," was the cheerful reply. "Here's a good warm fire. Take this armchair close to it, and don't remove any of your wraps till you cease to feel chilly. I should have prepared you some hot lemonade but for one little difficulty in the way: no lemons to be had. Coffee would keep you awake, but you shall have a glass of good, rich milk, either hot or cold, as you prefer. Now tell me what sort of a time you had."

"I wish every girl had such a mother as mine," Mildred said, smiling fondly up into the face she loved so well. "I verily believe I take as much pleasure in recounting my adventures to you as in going through them. And it so nice to have so safe and wise and loving a confidante.

Mother, I have a great deal to tell you, not so much about what has occurred tonight as of something that happened last night. I have been looking for an opportunity all day but without finding it, for we were so unusually busy all the morning and had company all the afternoon till it was time for me to get ready for the sleigh ride."

Mrs. Keith glanced at the face of a very tall, old-fashioned clock ticking in a corner of the room.

"I want very much to hear your story, daughter, but if you can sleep without having told it, I think we will reserve it till tomorrow, for it is now half past twelve!"

The girl would have been glad to unburden her mind and to learn if her mother approved—not of her rejection of Ransquattle, for of that there could be no doubt, but of the manner in which she did it— but that dear mother's face, cheerful though it was, told of physical exhaustion and need of sleep.

Mildred rose hastily. "High time then that we were both in bed. My story will keep perfectly well till tomorrow."

"Sit down and finish warming yourself by the fire," Mrs. Keith said with a smile. "I want to hear all about tonight. We will keep your longer story for tomorrow, then."

The Lightcaps found their house all dark. The family had retired to bed hours ago but had left the kitchen door unlocked and a good fire in the stove.

"Good and warm in here," remarked Gotobed, feeling for the candle and matches his mother was sure to have left on the table ready for them.

"Yes, feels comfortable. I shall set down and warm a bit 'fore I crawl up to that there cold bedroom."

"Me too. Don't expect to sleep none when I do get to bed," growled Gote, as he succeeded in lighting the candle after two or three ineffectual attempts and set it on the table again.

"Kind o' eggzited are ye?"

"Some. I say, what did you make room for that—"

"Don't swear," she sneered, as he paused for a suitable epithet to bestow upon Buzzard.

"I wa'n't agoin' to!" he said angrily. "Even though I've got sufficient cause in your letting that unclean bird in amongst us decent folks."

"There now. That'll do fer tonight," she snapped. "Tim Buzzard ain't no more an unclean bird than you are. He's twiced as good lookin' and sings like a nightingale, he does.

"But now, see here. Don't let's quarrel but go to work together to bring things round right. You don't want him to cut you out with Mildred Keith, and I don't want her to cut me out with him. So, now, you just spunk up and pop the question right off. If you don't, one or other o' them fellers'll get ahead o' you. You may just take my word for that."

Gotobed dropped his head into his hands and sighed deeply, then rose and walked the floor. Rhoda Jane watched him with an eager, half-contemptuous look.

"Well!" he said at length. "I wisht I knowed how!"

"Knowed how! You needn't make many words about it. 'Tain't like makin' up a sermon or a president's message."

"It's a heap more important—the happiness of a feller's whole life a dependin' onto it."

Silence reigned for some minutes, Rhoda Jane sitting meditatively before the stove with her feet on its hearth and her hands clasped round her knees, while her brother continued his restless walk.

She was the first to speak. "I'd write it out if I was you."

"I ain't used to writin' much."

"Well, you can get used to it. You can try and try till you've writ somethin' that'll do."

"I can't write anything good enough for her to see."

"Then take t'other way."

"I don't never git no chance, and if I did, I'd be tongue-tied, sure as the world."

"Then you'll have to write it, and I'll help you!" concluded Rhoda Jane with energy.

She arose as she spoke, picked up a candle, and stepped quickly to a corner shelf in the next room, from whence she brought an inkstand and a quill pen.

Setting these down on the kitchen table, she went back, opened a bureau drawer, and fished out from its depth a sheet of foolscap, which she spread out beside the inkstand.

"That ain't nice enough," said Gotobed, eyeing the sheet disapprovingly.

"Make it up on that, then get better at the store tomorrow to copy it onto," returned his sister. "Now, you set down and go at it like a man, or maybe I'd better say like a woman," she added sarcastically.

"If I'd only had an edication!" groaned Gotobed, taking up the pen. "It's mighty hard on a feller— such things as this is—when he hasn't got one."

"Well, do the best you kin, and mebbe it'll come out right for all. You're good-lookin' and got a good trade and can make a good livin' for her. Just tell her that and tell her you think she's as purty as a pitcher, and good-tempered, and knows a lot. Tell her you won't never let the wind blow rough on her, won't never say no cross words to her, and—and a lot more o' such stuff. That's what girls like."

"Well, I s'pose you'd ought to know, seeing you belong to the sect, but it's a heap easier for you to say that than it is for me to git it writ down in black and white," he sighed.

"I declare I'm clear beat out with you a'most," said Rhoda Jane, snuffing the candle impatiently. "I've a great mind to leave you to make it up yourself."

But she went on coaxing, suggesting, and prompting until, between them, they had composed an epistle which was satisfactory to her though not to her brother.

"It's nigh onto three o'clock, and I'm awful tired and sleepy," she remarked as at last they separated and sought their beds.

The next day, Gotobed searched the town for letter paper and bought half a quire of the best he could find.

During the next week, all his leisure moments were spent in making revisions to and improving upon his and Rhoda Jane's joint composition.

He had used his last sheet, and seized with a fit of desperation, he selected the one that seemed to him the least faulty and sent it by his sister.

Mrs. Keith, opening the door in answer to Rhoda Jane's knock, was suddenly struck with the peculiar expression of the girl's face—a mixture of pride, condescension, and exultation.

"Good evenin', Mis' Keith. Where's Mildred?" she said, stepping in and glancing about the room with an air of importance. "I want to see her pertickler; got somethin' fer her," and a conscious glance at the missive in her hand enlightened the quick-witted lady as to its nature.

"Mildred is not at home," she said. "She will not be until bedtime, but anything you choose to leave with me will be given to her upon her return."

Rhoda Jane considered a moment. She felt a strong desire to deliver the note into Mildred's own hand and to watch her while reading it. But should she carry it back, Gote might change his mind and put off indefinitely this business, which she was so desirous to have carried through at once.

She left it, though with evident reluctance.

She presently congratulated herself that she had done so. Gotobed, eagerly awaiting her return, peering anxiously every other minute through the smithy door, hailed her in breathless excitement.

"Well, what—what did she—"

"She wasn't there. She's gone out somewheres and won't be back till bedtime."

"Give it to me then, quick!" and he held out his hand with a peremptory gesture.

"I ain't got it," Rhoda Jane answered with a rather sardonic grin.

"Where is it? You ain't gone and left it?" he cried.

"Yes, I have. I give it to Mis' Keith."

Gotobed groaned. "I'd thought better of it. I'd throw it in the fire this minute if I had it here. She'll think me a fool. I know she will!"

"If she does, she's one," returned Rhoda Jane sharply, and she left him to his unavailing regrets.

How they tortured him! How could he possibly bear the suspense?

Mildred was merciful and did not keep him in doubt any longer than necessary. He found a letter next morning in the post office with his address on it and written in a lady's delicate graceful hand.

His heart seemed to jump into is mouth at the sight. He almost snatched it from the postmaster's hand, and without stopping to answer the jesting remark of that functionary on his sudden accession of color, he hurried away, never stopping till he reached the privacy of his own room—thankful that he succeeded in doing so without being seen by any of the family.

But now, it was a full minute before he could summon courage to open the missive and learn his fate. And even when it lay open before him, he passed his hand several times across his eyes as if to clear his sight.

Yet, it was very plainly written—also plainly expressed. It was a distinct, decided, though very kindly rejection of his suit. The only reason she gave was that she could not love him and that a loveless marriage could be nothing but misery to both parties.

# CHAPTER SEVENTEENTH

*The rose that all are praising*
*Is not the rose for me.*

—BAYLIR

"GOTOBED LIGHTCAP, you're the biggest fool that ever was born!" exclaimed the young blacksmith between his clenched teeth, throwing Mildred's dainty note upon the floor and grinding it with his heel, while the hot blood surged over his swarthy face, which expressed in every lineament his intense mortification and chagrin. "You might 'a knowed the likes o' her couldn't never fancy such a ungainly, know nothin' varmint as you be."

He dropped his face into his hands for a moment, groaning in spirit—for the wound in his heart was as deep as that to his pride.

"It does seem as if there warn't nothin' left in this world worth livin' fer!" he sighed. "But I'm not the feller to give up and die! I'll fight it out an' get over it yet."

He picked up the letter and thrust it into his shirt, straightened himself, went down into the smithy, and fell to work at his anvil, dealing vigorous blows as if thus he would drive away the demon of despair.

He ate very little at dinner, and conscious that

Rhoda Jane's sharp eyes were upon him, scarcely lifted his from his plate.

He hurried back to his work. She followed him the next minute.

"So, she's given you the mitten?"

"Who told you so?" he asked defiantly, standing before her with arms folded and head erect but reddening to his very hair.

"Humph! I ain't blind, and anybody could see it with half an eye. Well, never you mind! You're a sight too good fer her, the—"

"Don't call her no names now! I ain't agoin' to have it. It's me that isn't fit to hold a candle to the like o' her, and I had ought to had sense enough to know it.

"Besides, I didn't boast like Ransquattle. That's one small bit o' comfort as things has turned out," he concluded moodily, picking up his hammer.

"How'd he take his mitten?" laughed Rhoda Jane. "Wouldn't I ha' liked to seen him puttin' it on!"

"Take it! You never see anybody look so cheap as Nick when Mocker asked him t'other day when the weddin' was to come off. Then the fellers ragged him—'twas at Chetwood and Mocker's store where I'd run in on a arrant fer mother—and he growed thunderin' mad and begun callin' her names till Ormsby was ready to put him out. That is, if he hadn't stalked off hisself—and I could'a horse-whipped him with a right good will."

"Well, don't you go and break your heart fer her."

"I ain't agoin' to. There now, you'd better leave, fer I've got a job on hand."

The building lot selected by the Keiths was bought and fenced in almost immediately, and men were set to work at digging the cellar and then putting up the walls of the new house.

By dint of energetic oversight and urging on of the workmen, Mr. Keith succeeded in having it roofed in before the first heavy fall of snow, so that some advance could be made with the laying of floors, lathing, etc., during the winter.

When spring came, things took a fresh start. More men were employed, and every effort was put forth by the owner to have the building hurried to completion.

Each member of the family was deeply interested. The children made daily journeys to the spot, and all Rupert's leisure time was devoted to digging, planting, and other improvements of the grounds.

The boy was full of energy and fond of life in the open air. His garden did him credit, supplying nearly all the vegetables wanted for family use.

With some assistance from the older heads and hands, he terraced the bank overlooking the river, made steps down to the water's edge, where there was a fine spring, and there he built a small arbor and a spring house.

The new dwelling would be hardly so large as the one they were to leave for it until an addition should be built, but of more sightly appearance and far more conveniently arranged. Besides, it was their own, and who does not know the charm that ownership gives?

They were very impatient to get into it, and there was great rejoicing among the children when at last the announcement was made that it was finally fit for occupancy.

It was their father who brought the news into their reading and sewing circle one bright, warm afternoon early in July.

"When shall we move, wife?" he asked.

"Oh, tonight, tonight! Please, mother, say tonight," cried several little voices.

Mrs. Keith laughed. "It is not such quick work, my children."

"But we might bedin," said Don. "I'll take dis tat and tum back aden for other fings," he said, hugging a large white and yellow cat that had been a beloved member of the household for some months past.

"H'm!" said Cyril. "Toy can take his own self. He's got more feet to run with than any of the rest."

"And he always runs alongside wherever we goes," put in Fan. "Mother, can we help move?"

Her question to her mother was unheard and remained unanswered, for the reason that the older people were talking busily among themselves.

"I think we may begin tomorrow," Mrs. Keith said. "Celestia Ann is through her week's washing and ironing, and I'll set her and Mrs. Rood both to cleaning the new house while we pack up our things here."

"Oh, goodie, goodie! Mother, mayn't we all help?" chorused the children.

"We will see, dears. Perhaps there may be some little things that you can carry. Your own toys you shall carry at any rate, if you wish. Yes, Stuart, I have had the parlor and one bedroom of the new house cleaned already."

"Oh, mother," cried Mildred, "then can't we have this carpet taken up immediately—I mean go to work and take it up—and have it shaken and carried right over there? And perhaps we could get that done this afternoon, you and auntie and I, and have the furniture of that room carried right into it tomorrow morning, the first thing."

"A capital idea," her father said. "Then we will have one room comfortable there before all are torn up here. Come, children, scamper out of the way! Wife, where's the tack hammer?"

"Oh, can't we help?" pleaded the children. "Where shall we go?"

"No, not with this. Go anywhere out of the way."

The order was obeyed somewhat reluctantly, all going out to the adjoining room. Zillah and Ada stopped there, and each took a book. The younger three went upstairs.

"Let's pack up our things," said Cyril.

"What'll we pack 'em in?" queried Don.

"We'll see."

The boys both got out their stores of marbles, balls, bits of twine, a broken knife or two, a few fishhooks, and a set of Jackstraws their father had made for them.

Fan brought out her treasures also, which consisted of several dolls and their wardrobes, a picture book, and some badly battered and bruised dishes—

the remains of a once highly prized metal toy tea set.

A packing box in one corner of the large second-story room was where the playthings of the little ones were always kept when not in use. "A place for everything, and everything in its place" was one of the cardinal rules of the household.

"Can we take 'em over there now?" asked Fan, as she gathered hers pell mell into her apron.

"No, of course not," said Cyril. "Didn't you hear mother say we couldn't begin moving till tomorrow?"

"Then what did we get 'em out for?"

"To pack 'em up and have 'em ready to take over in the morning."

"What'll we pack 'em in?" reiterated Don.

"Let's look around for a box 'bout the right size," said Cyril. "Course, we can't carry them in the big board one. It's too heavy."

A good deal of rummaging followed upon that, first in the outer room, then in the other occupied by Aunt Wealthy and Mildred.

Finally, they came upon a pasteboard box standing on Mildred's writing table, which Cyril pronounced just the thing.

"But maybe Milly won't like us to take it," objected Fan, as he unceremoniously emptied the contents upon the table.

"Oh, she won't care. There's nothing in it but old papers and things writed all over. She's done with them, and she'll be puttin' them in the fire next thing. She always likes to burn up old rubbish."

That last statement was certainly according to fact, and Fan made no further objection.

Don suggested asking leave, but Cyril overruled that also. "No, they're all too busy down there. We mustn't bother," he said, walking off with his prize.

One paper had fallen on the floor. Fan stooped, picked it up, and looked at it curiously as the boys hurried off into the other room with their prize.

"Milly didn't do that," she remarked. "'Tain't pretty writing like hers. Guess she wouldn't want to keep such an ugly old thing."

"Come, Fan," Cyril called, "do you want to put your things in, too?"

"Yes," she said, coming out with the letter still in her hand.

Fan's dolls were put in last, and the box was too full to allow the lid to go on.

"I'll take Bertha and carry her in my arms," she said, lifting out her largest and favorite child. "I want her to play wis now, and I'd raser not trust her in dere wis dose marbles and balls rollin' round."

"Now the lid fits on the box all right," said Cyril, adjusting it.

"We're all packed up," observed Don with great satisfaction. "Now let's go play in the grove."

The others were agreed, and Fan decided that she must take with her two small rag dolls in addition to her beloved Bertha.

The cat had come upstairs with the children and was walking round and round them as they sat on the carpet, rubbing affectionately against them and purring loudly.

"Let's give 'em a ride on Toy's back," said Cyril. "Here's a string to tie 'em on with, and this old letter shall be the saddle," he said, picking up the one Fan had brought from the other room, which she had laid down beside the box.

The others were pleased with the idea. Cyril twisted the letter into some slight resemblance of a saddle, and in spite of a vigorous resistance from the cat, tied it and the dolls pretty securely to her back.

She was, of course, expected to go with or follow them as usual, but the instant they released her, she flew down the stairs and darted out of the open kitchen door, and scaled the fence in a twinkling.

The children pursued at their utmost speed, but Toy was out of sight before they could descend the stairs.

"Well, I never! That 'ar cat musta gone mad," Celestia Ann was saying, standing in the doorway with her hands on her hips and her gaze turned wonderingly in the direction Toy had taken.

"Where? Which way did she go?" asked the children breathlessly.

"Over the fence yonder, tearing like mad. She went like a streak o' lightnin' through the kitchen here, and I didn't see no more of her after she clum the fence. She's got the hydrophoby bad, you may depend, and I only hope she won't bite nobody, 'fore somebody knocks her in the head."

"No, it's my dolls she got," said Fan, who had not the slightest idea what "hydrophoby" might be. "Oh, boys, hurry and catch her 'fore she loses 'em," she called after her brothers as they renewed the pursuit, hurrying across the yard and climbing the fence with a speed that did credit to their ability in that line.

Fan stood beside it, gazing out anxiously through a crack between the high, rough boards till the boys returned all breathless from running to report, "No Toy and no dolls to be seen anywhere.

"But don't cry," added Cyril, seeing Fan's lips tremble ominously. "She'll come back when she wants her supper, you bet."

"It's wicked to bet," remarked Don virtuously.

"I didn't," said Cyril. "Let's go play in the grove. I'll bend down a tree and give you a nice ride, Fan."

Gotobed Lightcap had just finished a job, and pausing a moment to rest, he was wiping the perspiration from his brow with a rather dilapidated specimen of a pocket handkerchief when a cat darted in the open door, ran around the smithy in a frightened way, then lay down on the floor and rolled and squirmed, kicking its feet in the air in the evident effort to rid itself of something tied to its back.

With a single stride, Gotobed was at the side of the struggling animal.

He took it up and in a few seconds had relieved it of its hated encumbrance.

"It's them Keith children's pet cat," he said aloud, "and they've been a tyin' some of their doll babies onto it. There, you kin go, kitty. Don't take up yer lodgin' here, for we've cats enough o' our own.

"Eh! What's this?" he said as his eye fell on the letter, and he recognized his own awkward, all-shaped hieroglyphics.

He felt his face grow very red and hot as he straightened it out upon his knees, his heart fluttering with the thought of the possibility that it might have been some little liking for the writer that had prevented its immediate destruction.

There were some words written in pencil along the margin. He held it up to the light and slowly deciphered them.

He was not much accustomed to reading writing, and this had become slightly blurred, but he made it out clearly at last. It was a jesting remark about his mistakes in spelling and grammar, which were many and glaring.

"I wouldn't ha' believed it of her!" he exclaimed, crimsoning with anger and shame as he flung the torn and crumpled sheet into the fire of his forge, the dolls after it.

He caught his hammer and fell to work again, muttering to himself, "It's her writin'. There can't be no mistake, fer it's just like what she writ me afore. And I wouldn't a' believed it of her; I wouldn't. I thought she'd a kind heart and would make allowances fer them that hasn't had the same chance as her."

He had not been wrong in his estimate of Mildred. She would never have wounded his feelings intentionally. She had a habit of writing her thoughts on the margin of what she was reading, and the words had been carelessly traced there with no expectation that they would ever be seen by any eye but her own. Nor would they have but for the mischievous meddling of the children.

She set no value upon the letter and did not miss it till months afterward. She then supposed that she had destroyed it, though she could not distinctly remember having done so.

In the meantime, Gotobed kept his own counsel, concealing his hurt as well as he could and trying not to hate the hand that had inflicted it.

# CHAPTER EIGHTEENTH

*Farewell, a long farewell.*

THE KEITHS WERE scarcely more than well settled in their new home when Miss Stanhope announced her intention of returning to her home in Ohio almost immediately.

This news was received by the family with something akin to consternation. "How could they do without her?" they asked. "Didn't everybody need her every day of their lives, from father and mother down to Annis?"

"Ah," she answered smiling, though her eyes were dim with unshed tears, "you'll have each other and will soon find that you can get on very well indeed without your blundering old auntie. But the question is, how shall she do without you? The old Lansdale home will be very lonely with no little feet pit-patting about it."

"Then what makes you go, Aunt Wealthy?" chorused the children, clinging to her with many a loving caress.

"I must, my darlings. There's business I must attend to, and I feel that the ague is breaking me down."

"I fear that is too true," Mrs. Keith said with a strong effort to speak cheerfully, "and therefore I will not entreat you to stay, dear auntie. But rather, I urge your departure before the sickly season sets in.

"Though it just breaks my heart to think of the parting!" she added, hurrying from the room to conceal her emotion.

"But you'll come back soon. Won't you, auntie?" pleaded the children.

"Not very, I'm afraid, dears. It's a long and very expensive journey."

"Too long for you to take alone, Aunt Wealthy," said Mildred. "I dread it for you. I don't see how we can let you go without a protector."

"I shall not, child. Is not the promise to me, 'Behold, I am with thee, and will keep thee in all places wither thou goest?' Yes, to me and to each one of His children. So I am not afraid, and you need not fear for me."

"Dear auntie, if the Saviour were here, I think He would say to you, 'Oh, woman, great is thy faith!'"

"My dear, I deserve no such commendation; my faith is often very weak. But I want you to remember and try to realize that this almighty Friend not only goes with me when I leave you but stays with you also. According to His gracious promise, he says, 'I will never leave thee nor forsake thee.'

"Troubles and trials will come, and there are dark and stormy days in every life — but 'as thy days are, so shall thy strength be.'

"I cannot tell you, Mildred, how hard it is for me to leave you all," she continued, her voice trembling with emotion. "But it would be ten times harder were it not that I know 'this God is our God forever and ever' and that 'He will be our guide even unto death.'"

"Aunt Wealthy," said Mrs. Keith, coming in again, "Stuart and I have been talking this over—this resolve of yours to return to Ohio—and he says it will never do for you to attempt it without an escort."

"I shall be very glad of an escort, if there is one to be had," Miss Stanhope answered. "But if not, I must even go without—trusting in Providence."

"But you would wait a few weeks rather than go alone?"

"Certainly. God works by means, and we are to use them, while at the same time we trust only in Him."

"Stuart says the merchants will be going East to buy their fall goods. He will inquire among them and let you know."

"Ah, yes. I think I heard Mr.—um—what's his name? Mimicker? Sneerer?"

"Mocker?" suggested Mildred with a smile.

"Yes, yes, Mr. Mocker. I heard him say something about it being his turn this fall to lay in a new supply of goods."

"Ah, I hope it will turn out that you will have him for your escort, Aunt Wealthy," said Mildred. "I know that he will take the best possible care of you. But do try, auntie, to get his name fixed in your memory."

"That I will," Miss Stanhope answered with a good-humored smile, "for he might not fancy the synonyms of it, as the meaning not being the most complimentary in the world."

Mr. Keith brought home word that Mr. Mocker would leave for the East in a fortnight and would be happy to take charge of Miss Stanhope.

Aunt Wealthy had always been very dear to these nieces and nephews, but now that they were about to lose her, it seemed to them that they had never realized half her worth.

They lingered near her, they hung upon her words and looks, and when the time for parting came, clung about her with sobs and tears, loading her with caresses until she was forced to tear herself from their embraces and hurry away.

The stage had drawn up before the gate. She hastened down the garden path, the weeping children running after. Mr. Keith and Mr. Mocker assisted her into the vehicle, the latter took his place by her side, and in another moment, she was whirled away out of sight, drowning in tears and leaving the others in like condition.

"It seems just like a funeral!" sobbed Ada. "Oh, will she never, never come back anymore?"

"Perhaps she may, dear," said the mother, wiping her own tears. "We will try to think so at least and be cheerful and happy in looking forward to that time. Meanwhile, we may hope for a letter now and then."

"Oh," cried Rupert, "that reminds me! There's a letter in the office for you now, mother! I saw it there but had no money with me to pay the postage. If you'll give me two shillings, I'll run and get it now."

"Do so, my son," Mrs. Keith said, giving him the money. "I'm sorry you forgot it and did not get it out in time for Aunt Wealthy to see it."

Letters were rarities in those days, and the older members of the family awaited Rupert's return from the post office with a good deal of eagerness not unmixed with anxiety.

He was not long gone, for he, too, was curious in regard to it and desirous to learn its contents and the identity of the writer.

"It's postmarked Detroit," he said, delivering it to his mother. "I can't think who'd be likely to write to any of us from there.

"Unless it might be Captain or Edward Wells," he added with a quizzical glance at Mildred.

"The hand looks familiar," remarked Mrs. Keith, carefully breaking the seal, then, opening out the sheet. "Horace Dinsmore!" she exclaimed. "And he is coming to see us! Oh, what a pity that Aunt Wealthy has just missed him!"

"A pity, indeed!" echoed her husband. "But he may stay with us some weeks, and perhaps he can visit Lansdale on his way home."

"I hope he won't—won't stay here long, I mean," muttered Rupert in an aside to Mildred. "I didn't like him the other time."

"Nor I, very much, but perhaps he has improved."

"Mother, who is he?" the younger ones were asking.

"My cousin. His mother and mine were sisters."

"Were? Aren't they now?" queried Zillah.

"Yes, dear, but they both went home to heaven many years ago. My mother went first — before Aunt Eva married Mr. Dinsmore and went away down south to live.

"But wait till I have read the letter, and then you may ask all the questions you wish."

It was not a lengthy epistle. Mrs. Keith glanced over it and read it aloud. Its tone was cousinly and affectionate.

The writer stated that he had lately graduated from college and was now taking a tour to rest and refresh himself after many months of hard study. He said he had arrived in Detroit, would tarry there a week, and would then journey on into Indiana to visit his relatives in Pleasant Plains.

"This letter has been some time on the way," Mrs. Keith remarked, examining the date. "Really, I think he may walk in upon us day after tomorrow."

"Then we'd better be getting ready for him!" exclaimed Mildred, starting up in her energetic way.

"Wait a little. Mother promised to tell us about him," cried the children.

"Yes, I will. There's time enough, Milly."

Mildred resumed her seat, for she, too, wanted to hear all her mother had to tell.

"My mother," Mrs. Keith began, "was two years younger than Aunt Wealthy, who was the daughter of my grandfather by his first wife and therefore only a half-sister to my mother and Aunt Eva, who were the children of the second.

"Aunt Eva was five years younger than my mother

and still single when mother died, which, as you have all heard, was when I, her only child, was but little more than two years old.

"Cousin Horace, too, was the only child of his mother, and he was quite a little fellow when she died. I was there on a visit at the time and did what I could to comfort him.

"We grew quite fond of each other then and have always been so ever since, though we have lived far apart and have met very seldom."

"Has he got a father?" asked Cyril. "Does he live with him?"

"Yes, he has a father, and he lives with him when he is at home. But for years past, most of his time has been spent at school and college."

"I thought Cousin Horace had some brothers and sisters?" Rupert said inquiringly.

"Yes, his father soon married again and has a large family by the second wife."

"What is Cousin Horace like, mother?" asked Ada.

"Wait till he comes and see for yourself," was the smiling rejoinder.

"How glad you look, mother!" said Mildred. "Are you really so much pleased that he is coming?"

"Why, certainly, my child! He is my near kinsman, and as I have just told you, I am very fond of him. He's like a dear younger brother to me and particularly welcome just now as his coming will take away from the dreadfully lonely feeling Aunt Wealthy's departure has given the house."

"But, mother, we can't entertain him suitably. We're

so cramped for room, and our house is only half-furnished. He is used to living in such grand style. You know you have often told me about it—what a beautiful place Roselands is, and how many carriages and horses, and what a retinue of servants they keep."

Mrs. Keith smiled kindly at the anxious face turned toward hers. "Well, daughter dear, we'll just do the best we can for him, and it won't hurt him to try roughing it in the backwoods—or prairies, rather—for a little while."

"Well, it's a little better than if he had come while we were in the old yellow house. We've a nice porch here and a front yard shaded with grand old oaks, and there are no neighbors near enough to watch every movement."

"A good many conveniences, too," added her mother cheerily. "We've a beautiful view of river and town. I think, too, that we can manage to give him a room to himself and to feed him well, with the help of Rupert's garden, the cow, and the chickens."

The expectation of this visit was a real blessing to the family—to Mrs. Keith and Mildred especially— just at this time. It gave occupation to their thoughts as well as hands in the necessary preparation for the proper accommodation and entertainment of the coming guest, thus preventing much of the sadness the loss of Miss Stanhope's loved society would have caused them.

The next arrival of the semi-weekly stage brought Horace Dinsmore, his servant, and luggage to their door.

Mr. Dinsmore was a dark-eyed, handsome youth of distinguished appearance and with the air of a prince of the blood royal. Yet he was evidently a kind master, for his man, John, seemed to take the greatest pride and pleasure in waiting upon "Massa Horace" and anticipating his every wish.

While warmly welcoming her young relative, Mrs. Keith was somewhat dismayed at the unexpected sight of the servant, with house room being so scarce. But the difficulty was obviated by placing a cot-bed in the empty loft of the newly erected stable at the foot of the garden.

"How very thoughtless and selfish of Cousin Horace to bring that fellow along," Mildred said to her mother.

"No, my dear, not when you consider that they have always been together and neither would know very well how to do without the other. I was the thoughtless one not to remember that and expect John."

"Always together, mother?"

"Yes, they are nearly the same age—John a few months older than his young master—and were playmates in infancy.

"John's mother was Horace's 'mammy,' as the children down south call their nurses, and I think she may have loved her nursling even better than her own children.

"John's affection for Horace is probably as great, and it would come near to breaking his heart to be separated from him."

Horace Dinsmore had paid a visit to Lansdale the year before the removal of the Keiths to Indiana. The impression he had made upon his young cousins then was not favorable. He was silent, morose, and seemed to take little or no interest in anybody or anything.

"He is not like himself," Mrs. Keith had said to Aunt Wealthy again and again. "He is in trouble. Some great sorrow has come to him."

But they did not succeed in winning his confidence. He rejected their sympathy, locked up his secret in his own bosom, and left them as sad and as moody as when he had come.

He was changed for the better now. He was cheerful, at times even merry, and showed much interest in them and their affairs. He gave them valuable presents, for he had large means and a very generous nature.

Some gifts—of dress goods, jewelry, and children's toys—he had brought with him. In addition, he presented Mildred and Rupert each with a town lot in the immediate neighborhood of their new home.

Mr. Keith, in his sturdy pride of independence, was inclined to reject these last. But his wife said, "No, Stuart, do not. You will hurt Horace's feelings. The land is very cheap, and the price of it is nothing to him with his large wealth. I know it is a real pleasure to him to give it to the children."

Mr. Keith yielded the point and said nothing.

Mr. Dinsmore, not being a religious man and belonging to a very proud and aristocratic family, was not one to mingle with those he deemed "the common herd," and this his cousin well knew. Therefore, only a few of their acquaintances—the educated and refined—were invited to meet him and accompany them on little excursions—riding, boating, and fishing—that had been arranged for his entertainment.

He made himself agreeable on these occasions—an easy thing for him to do with his handsome person, polished manners, and good conversational powers. But soon, he let it be known to his relatives that he decidedly preferred exclusively family parties. After that, they had only such while he stayed, which was for several weeks.

# CHAPTER NINETEENTH

*Seldom shall she hear a tale
So sad, so tender, and so true.*

MR. HORACE DINSMORE showed much interest in Mildred, seemed to like to watch her, let her employment be what it might, and to have her company on long solitary walks and drives.

Several times he remarked to her mother that she was growing very lovely in person and was a girl with a fine mind, adding that he hoped she would not throw herself away upon some country boor.

The two—Mrs. Keith and Mr. Dinsmore—were alone in the sitting room one pleasant afternoon early in September when this remark was made for the third or fourth time. They were alone except that little Annis was playing about the floor, apparently absorbed with a toy and her doll.

Mrs. Keith was sewing, and her cousin, who had been pacing to and fro, now stood before her.

She lifted her head with a startled look.

"Horace, surely you don't forget that you and Mildred are cousins."

He colored slightly, then laughingly answered her thought rather than her words, "Don't be alarmed, Marcia. I'm not thinking of her in that way at all."

His face suddenly clouded over, as with some gloomy recollection.

"Marcia," he said, taking a chair near her side, "my visit is drawing to a close, and there is something I must tell you before I go. I came with the purpose of doing so, but hitherto my heart has failed me. We seem to be alone in the house, and perhaps there will be no better time than this."

"I think not," she said. "We can secure ourselves from intrusion by locking the door."

He rose, turned the key, and came back.

He did not speak again for a moment, but he sat watching Annis with a peculiar expression that excited his cousin's surprise and curiosity—and not for the first time either. She had noted it before: The child seemed to both attract and repel him.

More than once Mrs. Keith had seen him snatch her up suddenly with a gesture of strong affection, only to set her down the next minute and turn away as if from something far too painful to look upon.

"What is it you see in my baby, Horace?" she asked, laying her hand affectionately upon his arm.

"She is a sweet, pretty little thing, yet it gives me more pain than pleasure to look at her," he said, sighing and passing his hand across his brow.

"You cannot imagine why it should," he went on, smiling sadly into his cousin's wondering face. "because there is a page in my past life that you have never read."

His features worked with emotion. He rose and paced the floor back and forth several times. Then, coming to her side again, he said, "Marcia, I have been a husband. I am a father. My little girl—whom I have never seen—must be just about the age of Annis."

"You, Horace? You are but twenty years old!" she cried, dropping her work to look up at him in utter amazement.

"I knew you would be astonished—that you could hardly credit it—but it is true."

Then, resuming his seat, he poured out in impassioned language the story—already so well known to the readers of the Elsie books—of his visit to New Orleans three years before this, his hasty and clandestine marriage to the beautiful heiress Elsie Grayson, their speedy separation by her guardian and his father, the subsequent birth of their little daughter, and the death of her young mother, following so soon thereafter.

Her work forgotten, her hands lying idle in her lap, her eyes gazing intently into his, Mrs. Keith listened in almost breathless silence, the tears coursing down her cheeks during the saddest passages.

"My poor Horace! My poor, dear cousin!" she said when he had finished. "Oh, it was hard, very hard! Why did you never tell me before?"

"I could not," he answered in tremulous tones. "It is the first time I have spoken my darling's name since—since I knew that she was lost to me forever."

"Forever! Oh, do not say that! You have told me she was a sweet Christian girl, and none who trust in Jesus can ever be lost."

"But to me—I am no Christian," he sighed.

"But you may become one. The invitation is to you, 'Come unto Me;' and the blessed assurance, 'Him that cometh unto Me, I will in no wise cast out.'"

He sat silent, his face averted and his head bowed upon his hands.

She waited a moment, then spoke again.

"Your child, Horace?"

"She is at Viamede with her guardian."

"And you have never seen her?"

"No."

"Oh, how can you bear it? Doesn't your heart yearn over her? Don't you long to have her in your arms?"

"No. Why should I? She robbed me of her—of my darling wife."

"But you don't know that, and certainly it was innocently, if at all."

"That has always been my feeling."

"You ought not allow yourself to feel so," she said, almost indignantly. "Poor little motherless darling! Must she be worse than fatherless, too?"

"What would you have, Marcia?" he asked coldly, his face still turned from her. "What could I do with a child? She is well off where she is, better than she could be anywhere else. She is under the care of a pious old Scotch woman who has been housekeeper in the Grayson family for many years and that of her mammy, who nursed her mother before her and is a faithful old creature so proud and fond of her young mistress that I doubt if she would have hesitated to lay down her life for her."

"That is well so far as it goes, Horace, but do you wish your child to grow up a stranger to you? Would you have no hand in the molding of her character, the training of her mind?"

"I had not thought of that," he said, sighing, "but I do not feel competent to the task."

"But it is your work. It is a work God Himself has appointed you in giving you the child, a work for which He will give wisdom if you seek it of Him. 'If any of you lack wisdom, let him ask of God, who giveth to all men liberally and upbraideth not, and it shall be given him.'

"And if you neglect it, my dear cousin—bear with me, while I say it—it will be at your peril."

"How do you mean, Marcia?"

"The day may come when you will want that child's love and obedience, when you will covet them more than any other earthly good, and perhaps, you will find that they are denied you."

"It is possible you may be right in regard to the first," he said haughtily, his dark eyes flashing as he turned his face toward her again. "But as to the other—her obedience—it will be strange indeed if I cannot compel it. She may have a strong will, but she will find that mine is yet stronger."

"Horace," said his cousin earnestly, "if you refuse or neglect to do a father's duty by her, what right can you have to claim a child's duty from her?"

"I am not conscious of having neglected my duty toward her thus far," he said, still haughtily. "As I have already explained, she is where, in my judgment, she is better off for the present than she could be anywhere else. What changes may come in the future, I do not know."

"Forgive me if I have seemed to blame you so undeservedly," Mrs. Keith said with tears in her eyes. "But, ah, my heart yearns over that poor baby!"

She caught up her own and kissed her passionately as she spoke.

"Ah!" she sighed, pressing the little one to her bosom. "Whatever would my darling do without a father's and a mother's love!"

He walked to the window and stood there for several minutes. Coming back, he said, "Marcia, will you do me the favor and write about this to Aunt Wealthy? Tell her I have always felt ashamed of my behavior during my visit to you both two years ago. I could not bring myself to explain then the cause of my—what shall I call it? Sullenness? It must have looked like it to you and her and to all who saw me.

"But you will understand it now and perhaps have some charity for me."

"We had then, Horace," she said. "We were sure it was some secret grief that made you so unlike your former self. Yes, I will write to Aunt Wealthy. May I tell your story to Mildred also?"

"Not now, please. When I am gone, she may hear it from you."

"Excuse another question. Do you know anything of your little one's looks?"

"I have heard nothing, but if she at all resembles her mother, she must be very pretty."

"And you have never even asked! Oh, Horace!"

"I'm afraid you think me very heartless," he said, coloring. "But you must make some allowance for my being a man. Women, I think, feel more interest in such things than we of the sterner sex do."

"Then I think my husband must be an exceptional man, for he loves his children very dearly and takes great pride in their beauty and intelligence."

"I daresay. It might have been the same with me under happier circumstances," he answered bitterly.

Little feet came pit-patting through the hall, and little voices were asking for mother.

Mr. Dinsmore opened the door and admitted the inseparable three.

"Mother, I'm cold," said Fan, shivering, her teeth chattering as she spoke.

"Cold, darling? Come here."

"She's got a chill," remarked Cyril sagely. "I'm warm as toast. It's real hot in the sun where we've been playing."

"I'm afraid she has. Her nails are quite blue," Mrs. Keith said, taking one small hand in hers. "Come dear, mother will put you right to bed and cover you up nice and warm and give you something hot to drink."

"Me, too, mother," said Don, creeping to her side and laying his head on her shoulder. "I'm so tired and my head aches so bad."

His cheeks were flushed, his hands hot and dry.

"You, too, mother's little man?" she exclaimed. "Mother is so sorry for you both. Have you been cold, Don?"

"Yes, ma'am, and it creeps down my back now."

"Take care of Annis, Cyril," said Mrs. Keith, and excusing herself, she led the sick ones away.

Coming back after some little time, she sighed, "I found Ada down, too. She had crept away by herself without a word to anyone — poor, dear child! — not wanting to trouble mother, and there she lay, shaking till the very bed shook under her."

"It's dreadful!" cried Mr. Dinsmore, "positively dreadful, Marcia! How can you stand it? I believe there has hardly been a week since I came when you were all well."

"Ah, that's because there are so many of us!" she answered, laughing, though tears sprang to her eyes.

"Why do you stay here? I'd pack up everything and be off in an instant."

"Necessity knows no law," she said. "Cyril, son, can you go down to the spring and get some fresh water for the sick ones?"

"Yes, ma'am. I'll take the biggest bucket, cause folks always wants to drink so much water when the chills is on 'em."

"Cyril knows that by experience," his mother remarked as the boy left the room.

"Why do you speak of staying here as a necessity, Marcia?" asked her cousin. "You had as large a fortune from your mother as I had from mine."

"Riches take wings, Horace, and a large family and unfortunate investments supplied them to mine."

She spoke cheerfully, jestingly, as though it were but an occasion for mirth.

But his tone was full of concern as he answered, "Indeed, I never knew that. It is a thousand pities! I wonder that you can be so content and light-hearted as you seem."

"Ah, I have so much left! I have all of my chiefest treasures—husband, children, and many great and precious promises for both this life and the next."

"Ah, but if you stay here, how long are you likely to keep husband and children? Not to speak of the danger to your own life and health."

"Sickness and death find entrance everywhere in this sad world," she said, her voice trembling slightly, "and in all places we are under the same loving care. It seems our duty to stay here, and the path of duty is the safest. It is thought that in a few years this will be become a healthy country."

"I hope so, indeed, for your sake, but it is a hard one for you in other ways. I am not so unobservant as not to have discovered that you do a great deal of your own work. And I don't like that it should be so, Marcia."

"You are very kind," she answered, smiling up brightly into his face as he stood looking down upon her with a vexed and anxious expression. "It is very nice to have you care so much for me, Horace."

"There's nobody in the world I care more for, Marcia," he said. "And going over some of our late talk, in my mind, I have thought there is nobody to whom I should so much like to commit the care and training of my child. I mean, of course, if your hands were not already full and more than full with your own."

"They are not so full that I would not gladly do a mother's part by her," she answered with emotion, "were it not for the danger of bringing her to this climate."

"Yes, that is the difficulty. It would never do, as it is so cold and bleak during a great part of the year, especially for one born so far south. But I thank you, cousin, all the same."

"We have not much sickness here except ague," she remarked presently, "but there are several varieties of that—chills and fever occurring at regular intervals, generally every other day at about the same hour—dumb ague, shaking ague, and the sinking or congestive chills, which last are the only very alarming kind, sometimes proving fatal in a few hours."

"Indeed! You almost frighten me away," he said half seriously, half in jest. "That is not a very common form, I hope?"

"No, rather rare.

"Don't you send for the doctor?"

"Not often now. We did at first, but it is so frequent a visitor that we have learned to manage it ourselves."

The sickly season had fairly set in, and more afraid of the ague than he liked to acknowledge, Mr. Dinsmore hastened his departure, leaving for the East by the next stage.

# CHAPTER TWENTIETH

*I marked the Spring as she pass'd along,*
*With her eye of light and her lip of song;*
*While she stole in peace o'er the green earth's breast,*
*While the streams sprang out from their icy rest.*
*The buds bent low to the breeze's sigh,*
*And their breath went forth in the scented sky;*
*When the fields look'd fresh in their sweet repose,*
*And the young dews slept on the new-born rose.*

—WILLIS GAYLORD CLARK

"WELL, I'M BOTH glad and sorry Horace is gone," Mrs. Keith remarked with a smile, a sigh, and a dewy look about her eyes as the stage passed out of sight. "I'm fond of the lad but was troubled lest the ague should get hold of him. Besides, the dearest of guests is something of a burden with sickness in the house and a scarcity of help."

"Yes, that is very true, mother," Mildred answered. "So thoroughly do I realize it that I am wholly and heartily glad he's gone, albeit I liked him much better this time than I did before."

Celestia Ann had left months ago, and they had had very indifferent help during Mr. Dinsmore's visit, though fortunately such as they could keep away from the table when their guest was present at it.

Mildred went on now to express her satisfaction that such had been the case, adding, "What would he have done if Miss Hunsinger had been there and in her usual fashion asserted her right to show that she felt herself as good as he or anybody else?"

"He'd have annihilated her with a look," laughed Rupert.

"He would have acted like the perfect gentleman he is," said Mrs. Keith, "but it would have been exceedingly mortifying to me to have him so insulted at my table. For as he has been brought up, he could not avoid feeling it an insult to be put on a social equality with one so rude and vulgar."

"The house feels lonely," said Zillah. "It seems 'most as if Aunt Wealthy had just gone away."

"We'll get our sewing and a book," said her mother. "Come all into the sitting room. Rupert may be the reader this time.

"Mildred, you and I will have to be very busy now with the fall sewing."

"Yes, mother dear. It's a blessing to have plenty of employment. But do you think I shall need to give up my studies for a time?"

"No, daughter, I hope not. I certainly want you to go on with your studies. Mr. Lord says you are doing so nicely. Your cousin, too, told me he thought you were getting a better—a more thorough—education with him than you would be likely to in any boarding school for girls that he knows of."

Mildred's eyes sparkled, and Cousin Horace took a warmer place in her affections than he had held before. It was well, for it needed all that to keep her from disliking him for his indifference toward his motherless little one, when, a few days later, she heard his story from her mother's lips.

They had a very busy fall and winter, missing sorely Miss Stanhope's beloved companionship and her help in the family sewing, the putting up of fruit, the pickling and preserving—indeed in every department of household work, and in nothing more than in the care of the sick.

Letters came from her at rare intervals, for mails were infrequent in those days and postage was very high. Her letters were read and re-read and then put carefully by to be enjoyed again when the time and opportunity could be found for another perusal. They were not the brief statements of facts that letters of the present day generally are, but were long, chatty epistles, giving pleasing details of her own doings and those of old friends and acquaintances, and all that had happened in Lansdale since they left; telling of her pets, of the books she read, and what she thought of them.

Then there were kind inquiries, conjectures as to what they were doing and thinking, answers to their questions, and words of counsel and of tender sympathy in their joys and sorrows.

Many a laugh did they give their readers, and many a tear was dropped upon their pages. They so loved the dear old lady and could almost hear the sweet tones of her voice as they read and repeated to each other her quaint sayings.

Fall and winter passed, bringing with them no marked changes in the family but very much the same round of work, study, and diversion as in the former year.

The children grew, mentally and physically, with mother and as well as sister Mildred "teaching the young ideas how to shoot," for they could not endure the thought of resigning the precious darlings to the mercy of Damaris Drybread, whose school was still the only one in town.

The old intimacy was kept up in just the old way among the coterie of six, and the gossips vainly puzzled their brains with the question of which girl was the admired and admirer of which young man.

Mildred was happily freed from the visits of Ransquattle—of which Lu Grange had become the impatient and disgusted recipient—and saw little of Gotobed Lightcap, who, upon one excuse, or another, absented himself from most of the merry-makings of the young people.

Indeed, there had been scarcely any interaction between the two families since the removal of the Keiths from the immediate neighborhood of the Lightcaps, for there was no similarity of taste or common bond of interest to draw them together. There was nothing, in truth, save a kind and friendly feeling toward each other. And as regarded Rhoda Jane, even this was lacking.

She had not yet forgiven Mildred's rejection of her brother and almost hated her for it, though she knew naught of her added offense in the matter of criticism on his letter. That was a secret that Gotobed kept faithfully locked in his own breast.

Spring came early for that climate, with warm rains that brought vegetation forward rapidly.

The Keith children reveled in outdoor work and play. Each of the younger ones had a little garden to dig and plant as he or she pleased and a pet hen or two in the chicken yard. There was much good-natured rivalry as to who should have the earliest vegetables, the greatest variety of flowers, the largest broods of young chicks, or the most newly laid eggs to present father and mother or the invalid of the hour.

The old enemy, ague, still visited them occasionally—now one, now another, or it might be several at once succumbing to its attacks.

However, the lion's share of both gardening and poultry-raising fell to Rupert, who busied himself out of study hours with these and many little odd jobs of repairing and adorning—such as mending fences, putting up trellises, training vines, and trimming shrubbery and trees.

Mildred and her mother found so much to do within doors that some oversight and direction of these younger workers and the partial care of the few flowerbeds near the house were all they could undertake outside.

They had been without a domestic for some weeks and had passed through the trying ordeal of the regular spring housecleaning with only Mrs. Rood's assistance when one pleasant May morning, while dishing up breakfast, their hearts were gladdened by the sight of the sinewy form of Celestia Ann Hunsinger as she stepped in at the kitchen door with a characteristic salutation.

"How d'te, Mis' Keith? You don't want no help round here, do ye?"

"We want just the sort of help we'll be sure of if you'll take off your bonnet and stay," Mrs. Keith answered, giving her a hearty grip of the hand.

"Then that's what I'll do and no mistake," returned the girl, setting down a bundle on a chair with the remark, "You see, I've brought some o' my duds along," then pulling off her sunbonnet and hanging it on a nail. "Here, Miss Mildred, let me smash them 'taters.

"So Mis' Keith, you've been a buildin' since I was here last."

"Yes. A new kitchen, so we could take the old for a dining room and be less crowded."

"It's awful nice. I always did like a good big kitchen—room to turn around and keep things neat and straight."

"It's going to be nicer still, Celestia Ann," said Rupert, who had just come in from his work in the garden and was washing his hands preparatory to taking a seat at the table. "It wants a coat of paint on the outside, and I'm going to put it on myself today."

"Well, I never!" she exclaimed. "Do ye think you're up to that?"

"Of course I do, and so, I suppose, do father and mother, or they wouldn't have consented to let me try."

"Well, there's nothin' like tryin', as I've found out in my own experience," returned Miss Hunsinger, using her potato masher vigorously. "I allers enjoy meetin' with folks that's willin' fer it. But do you know, Mis' Keith, 'pears to me like 'I can't' comes the easiest to most human critters' tongues than any two words in the American language, and with more'n half on 'em, they're lyin' words. Yes, there's more lies told in them two words than any other ten. So there!" she declared as she laid down her masher to stir in the milk, butter, and salt.

"I'm afraid there is only too much truth in your remark," said Mrs. Keith. "Certainly, no one can accuse you of a fondness for that favorite phrase of the indolent and easy-loving."

"Thank you, Mis' Keith. I've lots of faults and failin's as well's the rest o' the human family, but I'm certain there ain't a lazy bone in my body.

"Here, these taters is ready to set on the table, and I see you've got your steak and biscuits dished up. But I hain't inquired after the fam'ly. Anybody got the agur?"

"No, I believe we are all well this morning, thanks to a kind Providence. Rupert, call your father and the rest to breakfast."

No frowns greeted Celestia Ann as she, with her accustomed nonchalance, took her place with the others. Everybody was glad to see her, because her arrival meant comparative rest for mother and Mildred and more time to be devoted by them to the loving care and entertainment of father and the younger children.

After breakfast came family worship. Then Mr. Keith went to his office, and the others scattered to their work or play. Sunbonnets and hats were in request among the little ones, for mother had given permission to go out if they would be careful to keep on the gravel walks till the dew was off the grass.

Sister Mildred gave kind assistance, and away they ran while she and Zillah and Ada, old enough now to begin to be useful about the house, made beds, dusted, and set things to rights in sleeping and dwelling rooms. Rupert donned a suit of overalls and went to his chosen task.

Celestia Ann needed but little direction or oversight, and in half an hour Mrs. Keith repaired to the sitting room.

What a pleasant place it seemed as she came in — fresh and bright from its recent cleaning and neat as a new pin, the open windows looking out upon the grassy side yard with its shrubbery and trees clothed in vivid green and giving a charming view of the clear waters of the swiftly flowing river sparkling in the sunlight.

"Isn't it a lovely morning, mother?" cried Mildred, whose graceful figure was flitting about here and there, putting a few finishing touches on the adornments of the room. "I think the sunshine was never brighter, the air never sweeter. It is a luxury just to live! Listen to that robin's song and the sweet prattle of the little voices you and I love so well! I feel as blithe and merry as a bird."

"Yes, dear child," said the mother, happy tears springing to her eyes. "Oh, how great is His goodness to us unworthy creatures—so much mercy and blessing here and the certainty of endless joy and bliss beyond! Life has its dark and dreary days, but after all there is more of brightness to those who look for it than of gloom."

"I believe that is true, mother," responded Mildred, "though when the dark and dreary days are upon us, it is sometimes very difficult to hold fast to one's faith.

"I do love this time of year," she added, leaning from the window to watch the ferryboat as it slowly crossed the river.

> *"Sweet spring, full of sweet days and roses,*
> *A box where sweets compacted lie."*

"Come, let us go out. I think we may spare an hour to the garden this morning," Mrs. Keith said merrily, leading the way. "What a blessing, among others, it is to have a good reliable girl in the kitchen!"

"Yes," laughed Mildred, "I could almost have hugged Celestia Ann, I was so glad to see her. What do you suppose has brought her back just at this time, mother?"

"Need of money for summer finery, I presume. Look, our morning glories are coming up nicely."

"Mother, mother and Milly," cried Fan, running to them in an ecstasy of delight. "My speckled hen has thirteen little chicks—the prettiest bits of fuzzy things you ever saw. Do come and look!"

She turned and fairly flew back again toward the chicken yard, mother and sister following.

The three other little ones were there watching "Speckle" and her brood with intense interest.

"See, see! Mamma, Milly, see! See!" cried Annis in a flutter of delight, holding her little skirts close to her chubby legs as the "bits of fuzzy things" ran hither and thither about her feet. "Pitty 'ittle chickies, dust tum out of eggs," she cooed.

"Yes, dears, they are very pretty," Mrs. Keith said, "but they are very tender little things, so be careful not to hurt them. No, Cyril, don't pick them up, and be sure you don't step on them. You may go to the house for some bread crumbs, Fan, and you and Annis may feed them."

This permission gave great pleasure, and Fan's small feet went skipping and dancing through the garden in the direction of the kitchen door.

Then mother had to look at Annis's hen sitting on her nest and notice how the older broods, which belonged to Cyril and Don, were growing in both size and strength—Zillah's and Ada's also—and hear how many eggs the other nests had furnished this morning.

After that, the gardens were submitted to her inspection, Mildred still bearing her company and both making suggestions and giving assistance.

And so a full hour had slipped by before they returned to the house, and Rupert, they found, had made great progress with his work.

"I've painted the whole end, mother. Do you see?" he called to her, 'and no, I'm beginning this side. I think I'll have the whole job done today."

"You have been very industrious," she said, "but don't make so much haste that it will not be done well."

"Oh, no, ma'am. I don't intend to."

He was at the top of his ladder and near the roof of the new one-story addition to their house.

"Take care, my son," said Mrs. Keith. "It seems to me your ladder doesn't stand very securely. Is there no danger of its slipping?"

"Never a bit, mother," laughed the boy. "Why, what should make it slip?"

She and Mildred turned and walked on toward the front of the house and had just set foot upon the porch there when a shout from Rupert startled them and made them pause and look back at him.

They saw the ladder slip, slip, then slide rapidly to the ground, while with a cry of alarm they rushed toward him.

But they were much too far to reach him in time to be of the least assistance. Down he came to the ground, falling with considerable impetus and alighting upon his feet, his brush in one hand, his paint pot in the other, striking with a force that sent the paint all over his person.

He reeled and dropped.

"Are you hurt? Oh, my boy, are you much hurt?" asked his mother tremulously, as she hurried to him, looking very pale and frightened.

"My clothes have gotten the worst of it, I believe, mother," he said, laughing and staggering to his feet. "I'm afraid they've robbed the house of half its new coat."

The other children came running from the chicken yard and garden. Celestia Ann poked her head out of the kitchen window, and a peal of laughter met him from all sides. "I dare say I cut quite a comical figure," he said, taking it in good part. "But since I've broken no bones, I wouldn't care a red cent, if it wasn't for the loss of the paint and the damage to my elegant attire.

"'Oh, what a fall was there, my countrymen.'"

"Since you are unhurt, no matter for the clothes, even if they were an elegant suit," said his mother with a sigh of relief.

"But half the paint's gone, mother—or at least put upon my person where it's worse than useless," the lad said, surveying himself with an expression so comically lugubrious that there was a fresh explosion of mirth.

"Never mind. It will not cost a great deal to replace it," said Mrs. Keith. "But I think the job may wait now till we can get a regular housepainter to finish it up."

"What! Would you have me give up so easily, mother, and own myself beaten? I don't like to do it.

Please let me try again, and I'll place the ladder more carefully."

"I don't know. We'll ask your father first. There's no special haste and—how would you all like to go with me for a walk? We can take a nice, long stroll down to the bridge and over the river to look for wild flowers."

The proposal was greeted with loud acclamations and clapping of hands. "Oh, delightful!" "Oh goodie! Goodie!" "May we, mother?"

"Yes. We've all been working hard this long time, and I think really deserve a holiday. Rupert, make yourself decent, and we'll set out at once, taking a lunch with us so that we need not hurry home."

"Tan I doe, mamma? Tan Annis doe?" asked the baby girl eagerly, the rosy face all aglow with delight at the prospect.

"Yes, indeed, mother's darling. You shall go in your little coach, because your dear little feet couldn't travel fast enough to keep up with the rest and you would get so tired."

"Do we need to be dressed up, mother?" asked Fan. "Me and Don and all the children?"

"No, dear. We don't go through town and are dressed quite enough for the woods."

They were soon on the way, strolling leisurely along and drinking in with keen enjoyment the sweet sights and sounds.

The sky over their heads was of a dark celestial blue, with here and there a floating cloud of snowy whiteness whose shadow flitted over the landscape, giving it a charming variety of light and shade.

Their road lay along the bank of the river, and its soft murmur mingled with the hum of insects and the song of birds. The grass beneath their feet was emerald green, thickly studded with wild flowers of every hue, and the groves of saplings through which they passed were fast donning their summer robes.

The bridge was a rough wooden structure half a mile below the town, quite out of danger of crowding the houses of the citizens or doing much injury to the custom of the ferry.

The walk was a longer one than the children were accustomed to take, but there was no occasion for haste. They were in search of rest and pleasure, and when little feet grew weary, mother let them stop and amuse themselves with making wreaths and bouquets of the flowers they had gathered or by throwing stones into the river until they were ready to go on again.

They did not go far beyond the bridge. They only climbed the bank on the other side, picked a few flowers there, and were ready to return home.

# CHAPTER
# TWENTY-FIRST

*You are meek and humble mouth'd;*
*You sign your place and calling, in full seeming,*
*With meekness and humility; but your heart*
*Is cramm'd with arrogancy, spleen, and pride.*

—SHAKESPEARE'S *HENRY VIII*

"OH, WHAT'S THAT? What's that?" cried a chorus of young voices as Mrs. Keith and her little troop, returning from their morning stroll, stepped onto the front porch at home.

"What, indeed!" echoed the mother, as much surprised as any one of the others. "It looks very like a box of goods, but where could it come from?"

"Aunt Wealthy," suggest Mildred, examining it with a curious eye.

"Ah, so you have come back at last, eh?" said Mr. Keith, coming out with a smiling face. "That's been waiting for you for over an hour," he added, consulting his watch. "Come let's have dinner, and then we'll see what's inside."

"Is dinner ready?" asked Mrs. Keith, taking off her bonnet.

"Yes, there's barely time for the washing of small hands and faces," he said, picking up Annis and racing off to the nursery with her—for so they called the room where the little ones slept and were dressed and undressed, though but a small part of the day was ordinarily spent there.

There was no lingering over the dinner table, though the meal was a good one, and the children's appetites had been sufficiently keen until they saw the box.

They ate and drank with dispatch, taking time for but little talk beyond a few conjectures as to its probable contents.

Father and mother certainly shared their curiosity and eagerness to some extent and did not keep them waiting long.

A few minutes' work with the hatchet, and the lid was off.

"Just newspapers!" cried Don in a tone of disappointment.

"Wait a bit, laddie," laughed Rupert.

"Something else underneath, I guess," said Cyril, while father, mother, and Mildred made haste to lift and lay aside the papers for further perusal. Newspapers were too rare in those days to be discarded, even though some weeks old.

"Books! Oh, delightful!"

"How good and kind of her!"

"Now, we'll have a feast!" exclaimed one and another in varying tones of gladness.

"What are they? Let us see," said Mr. Keith, proceeding to lift them out one or two at a time, and with a glance at the titles on the backs, he handed them to wife, son, or daughter.

"Cooper's *Naval History of the United States*! There, that will particularly interest you, Rupert.

"And here are his novels, which mother and Mildred will enjoy. Scott's works also—those for older folks and his *Tales of a Grandfather* for the children. Two more little books—*Anna Ross* and *Ruth Lee*."

"Oh, they look pretty!" cried Zillah and Ada, peeping into these last.

"*Dunallan* for me! Oh, how glad I am!" exclaimed Mildred the next instant.

"Here's a bundle," said Mr. Keith, handing it out.

"Remnants, I presume," his wife said laughingly. Opening it, she found her surmise correct.

Groceries, candies, and toys for the children, and some few other miscellaneous articles filled up the rest of this most welcome box.

"Dear old auntie! She shouldn't have wasted so much of her money on us," Mrs. Keith said with tears in her eyes as she glanced over a note pinned to a dress pattern for herself. "But she says she has enjoyed it intensely, and I know that is so, for giving—especially to us—is one of her greatest delights in this world."

"Yes, there never was a more generous soul," assented her husband.

"Ah, if we could only do something for her in return!" exclaimed Mildred.

"Yes, indeed! What a feast she has provided us!" cried Rupert, taking a peep here and there into the history book. "Mother, can't we begin on them this very afternoon?"

"I'm not ready for Mr. Lord," objected Mildred, "and in an hour it will be time to go to him."

That reminded the lad that he, too, had a lesson to prepare, and so he left the room to attend to it.

"Wife," said Mr. Keith, "do you know that little Mary Chetwood is seriously ill?"

"No, I did not. I'll put on my bonnet and go over there at once."

"Mother," said Mildred, "I've been thinking how it might be nice to lend one of these books to Effie Prescott. I do not know her at all intimately, but Claudina says she is very intelligent and fond of reading, and in such poor health that she is often too miserably weak and ill to do anything but read."

"Certainly! She may have the reading of every book in the house, if she wishes and will not abuse them."

"Claudina says that Effie is always very careful of those she lends her and is very glad to get them. She's a lovely Christian, too, and very patient under her trials."

"Yes. I have been pleased with the little I have seen of her. I believe I owe Mrs. Prescott a call, so I shall visit their house on my way to the squire's and carry a book with me."

Mrs. Keith found Mrs. Prescott out, the invalid girl lying back in a large rocking chair. Damaris Drybread seated, in her accustomed bolt-upright fashion, directly opposite.

At sight of Mrs. Keith, Effie started up in haste and trepidation to offer her hand, then a chair.

"Never mind, dear child, I will help myself," said the lady, pressing the trembling hand tenderly in hers. "How are you today?"

"About as usual, thank you, which is neither very sick nor very well," the girl answered with a faint smile, sinking back again and breathing very short and hard.

"Now don't talk so. You look very well," remarked Miss Drybread in a cold, hard tone. "Just make up your mind that there's nothing much the matter and you're not going to give up to the medicine, and ten to one it won't be long till you find yourself well enough."

Tears sprang to Effie's eyes, for she was both nervous and sensitive to the last degree.

"I know I look well," she said. "I'm not thin, and I have a good color, but it's often brightest when I feel the worst. And I've tried to believe my sickness was all in my imagination, but I can't. It's too real."

"No, Effie, you do not look well," said Mrs. Keith. "That brilliant bloom hardly belongs to health, and your eyes are heavy and your countenance distressed."

"Of course, she'll wear a distressed countenance as long as she imagines she's sick," observed the school-ma'am severely. "And you, Mrs. Keith, are only making matters worse by talking in that way."

"Not so," said the sick girl. "Such kind sympathy does me good. Oh, thank you a thousand times!" she said as Mrs. Keith put *Dunallan* into her hands. "I

235

shall enjoy it so much, and I will be very careful of it and return it soon. I read it years ago and liked it exceedingly, and it will be like new to me again now. Grace Kennedy is such a sweet writer. What a pity she died so early!"

"A novel!" sniffed Damaris. "If you are really sick, you oughtn't read anything but the Bible.

"The teachings of this book are so fully in accord with those of the Scriptures that I cannot think it will hurt her," said Mrs. Keith.

"I love the Bible," said Effie. "I never could do without it. Its words often come to me when I am sad and suffering and are 'sweeter than honey and the honeycomb.' But reading other good books seems like talking with a Christian friend, and it refreshes me in the same way."

At this very moment, Mrs. Prescott came in, and greeting the two callers with a pleasant "Good afternoon," she sat down to chat with them.

The talk presently turned to their gardens, and Mrs. Prescott invited the visitors to walk out and see hers.

Mrs. Keith accepted the invitation, but Miss Drybread said she would just sit with Effie till they came back.

"Aren't you teaching now, Miss Damaris?" asked the girl, as the others left the room.

"No, I've closed my school for a couple of weeks to do my spring sewing."

"It was kind of you to take time to call on me when you are always so busy."

"I try to attend to every duty," returned the school-ma'am with a sanctimonious air, "and I felt that I had a duty to perform here. I've been thinking a good deal about you, Effie. I've been trying to find out why your afflictions are sent, and I've concluded that it's as a punishment for your sins. I think that when you repent and reform, your health will be better.

"You know Christians—and I really hope you're one; I know you belong to the church—won't have any punishment in the other world, so they have to take it in this. And so, as I said, I've been consider-ing about you, and I think if you thought better of Brother Smith and enjoyed his sermons and prayers and talks in the meetin's, 'twould be better for you.

"He's a good Christian, and so you'd ought to like what he says and be his friend with other folks that isn't inclined to listen to him."

"He may be a Christian. I hope he is," returned Effie, "though it is very difficult for me to believe that a man can have much true love for Christ and for souls when his tone and manner seem to be utterly indifferent and businesslike. Or perhaps that isn't quite the right word, for men generally show interest in their business.

"Besides, it requires other things in addition to conversion to fit a man for teaching. He must have knowledge and the ability to impart it.

"I have nothing against Mr. Smith personally, but he does not instruct me, does not give me any food for thought, or help me on my way to heaven. So, I felt it my duty to object to having him become my pastor. But I haven't been going around slandering him, and I don't know why you come and talk to me in this way.

"It strikes me, too, that you should be the last person to do it—as I have heard you say far harder things of other ministers than I've ever said of him."

An angry flush rose in the cheek of the spinster.

"I've tried to do my duty always," she said, bridling. "I've never indulged in any vanities of dress, but that's been one of your sins, Effie Prescott, with your bows and even flowers and feathers on your bonnets and knots of bright ribbon at your throat and in your hair. It's sinful, and you may depend you'll be afflicted till you give up and be consistent in all things."

"I know better than you can tell me that I deserve all I suffer and a great deal more," said the girl humbly, tears gathering in her eyes, "but for all that, I don't believe you are right. You are like Job's comforters, and God reproved those men for talking so to him.

"And don't you remember what Jesus said about trying to take the mote out of your brother's eye while there is a beam in your own?"

"I see it's time for me to go," said Damaris, rising.

She stood a moment looking at Effie, her lips compressed, her face white, and her eyes ablaze with suppressed rage.

"There's no Christian spirit about you," she hissed. "You don't like faithful dealing. You don't want to be told of your sins. Very well, Miss, I wash my hands of you. I shake off the dust of my feet against you."

With arms folded on her breast and head erect, she stalked out of the house, leaving the invalid girl quivering from head to foot with nervous excitement and distress, crying and laughing hysterically.

"Oh dear! Oh dear!" she sighed to herself. "I haven't behaved in a Christian manner. I was angry at what she said."

Mrs. Prescott and Mrs. Keith were strolling in from the garden, chatting pleasantly of their domestic affairs, when an infant's screams were heard coming from the back room.

"There, my baby is awake and calling for his mother," said Mrs. Prescott. "Please excuse me a minute. Just step into the parlor again and talk with Effie, if you will."

Mrs. Keith complied and found Effie alone, lying back in her chair, trembling, flushed, and tearful.

"My poor child! Are you suffering very much?" she asked, bending over her and smoothing her hair with a caressing motion.

"No, ma'am, I'm not worse. It was something that Damaris said, and I didn't take it quite as I ought.

"Oh, Mrs. Keith, do you think that God sends sickness to punish us for our sins and that my health is poor because I'm more wicked than anybody who is well?"

"Certainly not. I have excellent health as a general thing, while many an eminent saint has been a great sufferer.

"We know that sin brought disease and death into the world and that God sometimes sends afflictions as chastisements, but to his own people it is in love and for their growth in grace.

"'As many as I love, I rebuke, and chasten; be zealous therefore and repent.' 'Whom the Lord loveth he chasteneth, and scourgeth every son whom He receiveth. If ye endure chastening, God dealeth with you as with sons.

"Remembering that, would you wish to escape it?"

"Oh, no, no! But oh, it makes the burden so much heavier to think that it is because He may be angry with me!"

"It is because He loves you. Do not look at this as punishment but as discipline. It is the cutting and carving which are necessary to bring out the beautiful statue from the shapeless block of marble or to change the diamond in the rough into the brilliant gem.

"As to the idea that the Christian bears any part of the penalty of his sins—atoning for them by his own suffering, or his works, or in any other way, either in this life or the next, it is totally unscriptural. 'For Christ is the end of the law for righteousness to every one that believeth.'"

"Oh, thank you so much, so very much!" she exclaimed, looking up gratefully. "What wonderful love His was, and who would not be willing to bear any suffering to be made like unto Him?"

"That is unquestionably a Christian spirit," said Mrs. Keith. "None but those who have felt the burden of sin and learned to hunger and thirst after righteousness know that ardent desire for conformity to His image."

"You make my heart glad!" cried the girl. "Damaris just told me there was no Christian spirit about me—and I'm often afraid there isn't—yet I do love Jesus and desire His love more than anything else. I want to do and suffer all that is His holy will!"

Little Mary Chetwood, a sweet child of six, was the only daughter except Claudina, and coming after some half a dozen boys, naturally became from the first a great pet and darling. She was made much of by parents, sister, and brothers.

Yet she was not a spoiled child; she had been taught obedience, religiously trained, and not so indulged as to hurt her.

Love and wise indulgence do no harm; quite the contrary. But harshness, a dearth of affection, and undue severity have ruined many a one for time and eternity.

Mrs. Keith found the Chetwoods a distressed household, for though the little girl had been but two days ill, such was the violence of the attack that it was already apparent that there was only a small hope of recovery.

"This is kind," whispered Mrs. Chetwood, pressing her friend's hand, while tears coursed down her cheeks. "The darling won't be tended by anybody but mother, father, or sister, but your very presence is a great comfort."

"I would have been here sooner, but I did not know of her illness till this afternoon," Mrs. Keith responded in the same subdued key. "If I can be of any use, I will take off my bonnet and stay. It is perfectly convenient."

The offer was gratefully accepted, and a note was dispatched to Mildred, entrusting the children at home to her care till such time as her mother could be of no more service at the squire's, and Mrs. Keith's gentle ministries in the sick room began.

Her quiet movements, her thoughtfulness, quick comprehension, and abundance of resource made her invaluable at such a time.

The end came sooner than was expected. Day was just breaking when, with her head on the bosom of the one who gave her birth, the little one gently breathed her last.

In all the trying scenes that followed, Mr. and Mrs. Keith and Mildred were most kind, helpful, and sympathizing, and the ties of Christian fellowship were thus more closely drawn than ever between the two families.

The bereaved family found their home sadly desolate, but there was no murmuring against the Hand that dealt the blow. The language of their hearts was, "The Lord gave, and the Lord hath taken away. Blessed be the name of the Lord."

# CHAPTER
# TWENTY-SECOND

*Hail! independence, hail! Heaven's next best gift,*
*To that of life, and an immortal soul.*

—THOMSON

*There is strength,*
*Deep bedded in our hearts, of which we reck*
*But little till the shafts of heaven have pierc'd*
*Its fragile dwelling. Must not earth be rent*
*Before her gems are found?*

—MRS. HEMANS

"BOOM!"

The loud voice of the cannon rent the air with sudden shock just as eager, waiting eyes caught the first glimpse of the sun's bright disc peeping above the eastern horizon.

The sound broke suddenly in upon many a dream, woke many a sleeper.

"Independence day! The glorious Fourth, the nation's birthday," shouted Cyril, giving Don a kick and springing out of bed and hurrying on his clothes.

243

"Oh, oh! Fourth of July!" echoed Don, following suit. "I'm so glad, 'cause now we can fire our crackers, Cyril."

Their clatter and another shot roused Fan and Annis, who joined in the rejoicing, the latter calling loudly for mother or Milly to come and dress her.

"No more hope of sleep," yawned Mr. Keith in the next room, "so we may as well get up."

"Yes," returned his wife, "I wish you would, and watch over the children—see that they don't burn their fingers or set things on fire.

"Yes, Annis, mother is coming."

Breakfast was prepared amid the almost constant firing of crackers and childish shouts of exultation, near at hand, and the occasional booming of the more distant cannon.

The young folks were full of merriment and great excitement, hurrahing, and the singing of *Yankee Doodle,* the *Star-spangled Banner,* and *Hail Columbia!*

Rupert came in a little late to breakfast from a stroll through town, and he reported that a wonderfully large flagstaff had been planted in front of the courthouse and that the Stars and Stripes were floating from its top.

The Sunday schools were to unite and march in procession through the streets of the town, then separate, and each group go to its own church to there enjoy a little feast prepared by the parents and friends of the scholars.

There had been a good deal of baking going on in Mrs. Keith's kitchen the day before, and shortly after breakfast a large basket was packed with delicacies and sent to the church.

Mildred and her mother had their hands full for an hour or so in dressing the children and themselves in all their finery for the grand occasion.

They made a goodly show as they issued from the gate and made their way toward the place of rendezvous. The girls were all in white muslin and blue ribbons, and the boys were in their neat Sunday suits, each with a flower or tiny nosegay in his buttonhole.

The house had to be shut up, as Celestia Ann claimed the holiday, but it was left in its usual neat and orderly condition by means of early rising and extra exertion on the part of the three older girls. Otherwise, Mildred would not have been content to go, and delay was dangerous because the procession, in an effort to avoid the worst of the day's heat, was to move by nine o'clock.

The whole town was in grand holiday attire, and everywhere smiling faces were seen.

A shower in the night had settled the dust without turning it to mud, and the Sunday school celebration proved quite a success.

The children enjoyed their treat of cakes, candies, and lemonade, then the little Keiths went home, tired enough to be glad to sit down and rest while father, mother, and Milly told them stories of other Fourths that they could remember.

After dinner, Mildred went to call on her friend Claudina, carrying with her another book for Effie Prescott.

*Dunallan* had been returned in perfect condition and with a little note of thanks to the Keiths for their kindness in lending it.

Effie met Mildred with a pleased look, a cheerful greeting, and warm thanks for the book.

"I am so glad to see you!" she said. "It was very kind of you to come, for I am owing you a call. I thought I should have paid it long ago, but there are so many days when I don't feel quite equal to the walk."

"You do walk out then?"

"Oh, yes, every day when the weather is good. That is part of the cure. But I cannot walk fast or far."

"I hope you are improving."

"Yes, I believe so, but very slowly. I'm never confined to bed but never able to do much. The books are such a blessing."

From that, they fell into talk about books and authors and were mutually pleased to find their tastes were similar with regard to literature and that their religious views accorded.

It was the beginning of a friendship that became a source of great enjoyment to them both.

Effie had learned to love Mrs. Keith. That drew Mildred toward her, and their common faith in Christ and love of Him was a yet stronger bond of union.

They regretted that they had been so long comparative strangers, and Mildred felt well rewarded for the kind thoughtfulness on her part, which had at length brought them together.

But leaving Effie to the perusal of the book, she walked on to Squire Chetwood's.

Mrs. Chetwood and Claudina, wearing their deep mourning dress, sat quietly at home and had no heart to join in the mirth and jollity going on about them. Yet, they seemed calm and resigned.

"Ah," sighed the mother, tears springing to her eyes as the joyous shouts of children penetrated to their silent room, "our little darling would have been so happy today! But why do I say that? I know she is far, far happier in that blessed land than she could ever possibly have been here."

"I know that," said Claudina, weeping, "and I do rejoice in the thought of her blessedness. But oh, the house is so dreary and desolate without her! Oh, Mildred, how rich you are with four sisters!"

There was a knock at the street door, which was answered by the girl, and the next moment Miss Drybread walked into the parlor where the ladies were sitting.

She was courteously received and invited to take a seat, which she did, as she drew a deep sigh.

"Are you well, Miss Damaris?" asked Mrs. Chetwood quietly.

"Yes. I'm always well. I try and do right, and I have no sick fancies. I am never troubled with the vapors. I hope you're well?"

"As usual, thank you."

"You've had a great affliction."

No response, for the torn hearts could scarcely endure the rude touch. Her tone was so cold and hard.

"I hope you're resigned," she went on. "You know

we ought to be, especially considering that we all deserve our troubles and trials."

"I trust we are," said Mrs. Chetwood. "We can rejoice in her happiness while we weep for our loss."

"Don't you think you made an idol of that child? I think you did and that that is the reason why she was taken, for God won't allow idols."

"We loved her very dearly," sobbed the bereaved mother, "but I do not think we made an idol of her or even indulged her to her hurt."

"The heart is deceitful," observed the schoolma'am with emphasis. "And putting on mourning and shedding so many tears doesn't look like submission and resignation. I don't see how Christians can act so."

"Wait till you are bereaved," replied the mother, sobs almost choking her utterance.

"And remember how Jesus wept at the tomb of Lazarus. He never reproved the Jews for putting on sackcloth and ashes when mourning for their dead," said Mildred, adding, in her uncontrollable indignation, "I think you might be at better work, Miss Drybread, than wrenching the hearts of these bereaved ones whom Jesus loves and in all whose afflictions He is afflicted."

"I'm only doing my duty," retorted the spinster. "The Bible says we must reprove our brethren and not suffer sin upon them."

"It says, 'Judge not, that ye be not judged.' They are the words of Jesus in the Sermon on the Mount, and if you turn to the passage and read on a little further, you will see that He calls hypocrites those people who try to pull the mote out of a brother's eye while there is beam in their own."

"I can understand an insinuation as well as the next one," said Miss Drybread, rising in wrath, "and let me tell you, Miss, that I consider you the most impertinent young person I ever met.

"Good afternoon, Mrs. and Miss Chetwood. I wish you the joy of your friend," and she swept from the room and the house before the astonished ladies could utter a word.

"What an entirely disagreeable, self-righteous old hypocrite!" cried Mildred, her cheeks flushed, her eyes flashing. "To think of her talking to you in that cold-hearted, cruel manner, Mrs. Chetwood and Claudina. But there! I am judging her. Oh, dear!"

She finished with a burst of sobs, clasping her arms about her friend, who was weeping bitterly.

Mrs. Chetwood, too, was shedding tears but presently wiped them away, saying, "We will try to forgive and forget her harsh words. I trust she is a well-meaning, and perhaps truly good woman, though mistaken as to her duty and sadly wanting in tact."

On her way home, Mildred passed the Lightcaps' house. She usually avoided doing so by taking the other street, but today she was too full of grief for her bereaved friends to even care which way her steps were tending till they were arrested by Mrs. Lightcap's voice, speaking from her door.

"Why, if it ain't Miss Keith! I hain't seen a sight o' you this long time. Walk in, won't you, and sit a bit? They've all run off somewheres and left me settin' here without a soul to speak to, and I'm dreadful lonesome."

Mildred could not politely refuse the invitation, and so stepped in and took a seat.

Her first feeling on becoming aware that Mrs. Lightcap was addressing her was one of embarrassment at the idea of facing the mother of her rejected suitor. But the next instant she concluded from the cordial manner of her neighbor that she must be entirely ignorant of the affair, which was really the case. Gotobed had insisted upon Rhoda Jane keeping his secret.

Mildred was not in a talking mood, but Mrs. Lightcap grew garrulous over the day's celebration, the heat of the weather—prophesying that if it lasted long, coming as it did after a very rainy spring, there would be a great deal of sickness—and branching off finally to her housework and garden, which were two inexhaustible themes with her.

An occasional yes or no or nod of acquiescence was all that was necessary on the part of her listener, and these Mildred could supply without giving her undivided attention to the steady flow of empty talk.

The firing of the cannon at short intervals had been kept up all day. "Boom!" it came now, causing Mrs. Lightcap to give a sudden start and break off in the middle of a sentence.

"Well, I declare!" she exclaimed. "I can't git used to that there firin'. I jest wisht they'd stop it 'fore some on 'em gits hurt. It's a dreadful dangerous thing, gunpowder is, and I guess there ain't never a

Fourth goes by when there don't somebody git about half killed."

"Or quite," said Mildred. "People can be so careless, and I suppose that even with the greatest care there must be some danger from the bursting of guns and other accidents that it is, perhaps, impossible to guard against."

Mildred sat very near the open door, Mrs. Lightcap farther within the room.

"Well, as I was sayin'," began the latter, resuming the thread of her discourse.

Someone came running without, his very heavy footsteps resounding upon the sidewalk. It was a man. He paused before the door, looking pale and frightened, then beckoning to Mildred, said in a low, hurried tone, "Just step this way a minute, Miss. I want to speak to you."

Hardly comprehending and too much taken by surprise even to wonder what he could want, she hastily complied.

"She ought to be prepared, you know," he went on in the same breathless, agitated manner, drawing her farther away from the door as he spoke. "He's awfully hurt, a'most killed, I believe, and they're bringin' him up the street now."

"Who?" gasped Mildred.

"Her son Gote. The gun went off while he was ramming in the wadding. It shot the ramrod right through his hands. I guess they'll both have to come off."

Mildred staggered back, sick and faint and with a dazed sort of feeling that she was somehow to blame.

"They're comin'," repeated the man hurriedly, pointing to a little crowd of men and boys moving slowly up the street, scarcely a square away. "Can't you say something to her? Kind 'o break the shock a little, you know?"

Mrs. Lightcap had stepped into the doorway and was looking this way and that, curious to learn the cause of Mildred's sudden exit.

"Why, Jim Foote, is that you?" she exclaimed. "What on airth are you a wantin' with Miss Keith?" Then, catching sight of the slowly approaching crowd, she inquired, "What's goin' on? Anything the matter?"

Mildred sprang to her side and fairly pushed her back into the house. She threw her arms about her, sobbing, "Oh, I'm so sorry for you! So sorry! Don't look! Not yet. He—he's living, but—"

"Who? Who's a livin'? Who's hurt? Girl, tell me quick! 'Tain't my old man? Oh, what'll I do? What'll I do?"

The tramping of many feet drew near to the house. Her husband rushed in, pale, breathless, and trembling, and at the sight of his wife burst out crying like a child. Then the wounded man was supported into the house, with men and boys and even women and girls crowding in after, until shortly the room was full.

Rhoda Jane and the younger brothers and sisters were there, screaming and crying. Gotobed was silent, bearing his agony with the heroism of a soldier, but as his mother caught sight of his ghastly face, his mangled hands, the blood upon his person, and the surgeon with his instruments, she uttered a wild shriek and fell back fainting.

Her husband carried her into the kitchen, and some of the neighbor women gathered around her with restoratives and whispered words of pity and condolence, while others hurried back and forth in quest of such articles as the surgeon called for.

Rhoda Jane rushed out the kitchen door and ran to the foot of the garden, screaming and wringing her hands, the younger ones following her.

Mildred could not go away and leave the family in their dire distress. She caught Gotobed's eye, and there was in it a dumb entreaty that she had neither the power nor the heart to resist.

Silently she made her way to his side. The doctors were clearing the room of all who were not needed.

"They're a goin' to take off my right hand," he said hoarsely. "It's an awful thing, but if—if you'll stand by me and let me look in your eyes, I can bear it."

She turned hers upon the surgeon, Lucilla Grange's father.

"May I?"

"If you have the nerve, my dear child. It would be a great kindness to the poor fellow. There ought to be a woman near him, and it seems neither mother nor sister is equal to the task."

"I will stay," she said, a great compassion filling her heart. "I shall not look at what you are doing, but I will stand by and fan him."

She kept her word, forgetting herself entirely, thinking of him only as one suffering terrible agony and in need of her support. She stood gazing into his eyes and in her heart sent up silent, fervent prayer on his behalf.

Chloroform and ether were not known in those days, and the knife's cruel work must be borne without the blessed insensibility to pain that they can give. Had the magnetism of Mildred's gaze a like effect? I know not, but something enabled Gotobed to pass through the terrible ordeal without a groan or moan, almost without flinching.

The right hand had to be taken off at the wrist. The left, though much mangled, the surgeon hoped to save, and he did so ultimately.

The amputation and the dressing of the wounds was over at last, and Mildred was turning away when a cup of tea was put into her hand with the words, spoken in a half whisper, "Give him this; he will take it from you."

She held it to his lips, and he drank. A plate was silently substituted for the cup, and she fed him like a child.

Poor fellow! It would be a long time before he could feed himself again.

Mildred set down the plate and stole quickly from the house. Her long pent-up emotions must find vent.

She went weeping home, her heart breaking with pity for the man she could not love and could not have married for the wealth of the world. Oh, why did he love her so?

She had read it in his eyes—that she was more to him than all the world and that he knew his was a hopeless passion.

She was glad to see that the sun was setting, because she knew from the lateness of the hour that tea must be over at home and the little ones in bed. She dreaded their questionings and curious looks and loathed the thought of food.

Her mother, that best earthly friend who always understood her as by intuition, met her at the door and clasped her in a tender, loving embrace. On that dear bosom the whole sad story was sobbed out.

"Poor, poor fellow! My heart aches for him," Mrs. Keith said, mingling her tears with Mildred's. "And, my dear child, I am very glad you had the courage and firmness to give him the help you did. I pity him, too, for his unfortunate attachment, while at the same time I could never, never be willing to see it returned, Mildred.

"But your courage surprises me. I doubt if I should be capable of the like myself," she added, smiling through her tears.

"I know you would, mother dear," returned the girl, gazing with loving admiration into her mother's eyes. "You are far braver and firmer than I. I should not have expected to be able to do it myself, but we never know what we can do till we are tried.

"I am sure our Father helped me in answer to prayer and according to His gracious promise, 'As thy days are, so shall thy strength be,'" she added in subdued, tremulous tones.

"I do not doubt it," said Mrs. Keith, "for 'our sufficiency is of God.'"

Throughout the whole town, great sympathy was

felt for the wounded young man. People showed it in various ways: by inquiries made of the doctor or at the door, by stopping by for a little friendly chat, and sending delicacies to tempt his appetite, which for a time failed under the pressure of pain, enforced idleness—a great change for one who had been all his life a hard worker—and depression of spirits. There were seasons when he was well-nigh overwhelmed at the thought of his maimed and helpless condition.

Mrs. Keith went frequently to see and comfort him and his distressed mother, and she was more successful in so doing than almost anyone else, except Mildred, who occasionally accompanied her.

They carried to Gotobed food for the mind as well as the body—books which they read to him, as he could not hold them himself and the other members of the family had little time or ability to entertain him in that way.

Also, they said many a kind and encouraging word concerning the possibilities of future usefulness yet remaining to him.

"I shall never be good for nothing no more," he sighed mournfully one day, looking down at his maimed arm and wounded hand. "I can never swing my hammer or shoe a horse again. I'll have to be a helpless burden on other folks, 'stead o' takin' care o' father and mother when they git old, as I used to think I should."

"I don't know that, Gotobed," Mrs. Keith answered cheerily." I think God has given you a good mind and that you will gradually learn to do a great deal with that left hand. You will be able to write, hold a book, or turn the leaves, and so you may be able to educate yourself for usefulness in some new line—perhaps do more for your parents and friends than you ever could have done with your hammer."

A light broke over his face at her words, "Oh!" he said, drawing a long breath. "If I thought that, I could bear it."

"I think you are bearing it bravely," she said.

"I'm tryin' my best," he sighed, "but the Lord only knows how hard it is—'specially when folks comes and tells you it's a judgment sent onto you for your bad sins."

"And who dares to tell you that?" she cried, flushing with indignation. "Who on earth could be so heartlessly cruel?"

"Well, Damaris was in t'other day. She means well enough, I guess. She fetched something she'd cooked up for me, but she don't seem to understand a feller critter's feelin's. She give me a long lecture; said I'd been dreadful proud of my strength and what a neat job I could make o' shoein' a horse and the like, and so the Lord took away my hand to punish me and fetch me down. Do you think 'twas that way, Mis' Keith? I was thinkin' 'twas my own carelessness and not to be blamed on Him at all."

"It strikes me that you are very nearly right there," she replied, half-smiling at the earnest simplicity with which he spoke. "He is very merciful and gracious, full of tender pity and compassion for the creatures

He has made, especially those who are peculiarly His own because they have accepted the salvation offered through Christ Jesus. Yet He does not always see fit to save them from the consequences, as regards this life, of their own follies and sins."

"Carelessness is a sin," he said with a heavy sigh. "I didn't used to think so, but it's plain enough to me now. And do you think, Mis' Keith, He feels kind o' sorry for me even though 'twas my own fault?"

"I am sure of it and that He will give you strength to bear your trouble if you will ask Him, to bear it bravely and not let it spoil your life by robbing you of cheerfulness and hope and the usefulness you may attain to by a determined, manly struggle with your difficulties.

"There is a pleasure in overcoming difficulties," she added with a bright, winning smile that was like a ray of sunlight to his saddened heart, "a pleasure that the slothful know nothing of."

"I'll try it!" he said with determination. "God helping me, I will. Bless you, Mis' Keith, fer them words. I'll never forget 'em."

# CHAPTER TWENTY-THIRD

*The sad vicissitude of things.*

—STERNE

"MY POOR, DEAR friend, would that I could comfort you!" Mrs. Keith said in tones of deep heartfelt sympathy, folding her arms about Mrs. Chetwood and weeping with her. "But only Jesus can do that in such sorrow as yours."

"And He does, else I should die, for my arms are so empty and my heart and home so desolate!" sobbed the bereaved mother.

"I know it; I know it by sad experience, for I, too, have wept over the grave of a darling little one."

"You?" Mrs. Chetwood said with a look of great surprise. "You have so many."

"Yes, but then I had not all I have now. Eva was between Rupert and Zillah and would be thirteen now. She was five when God took her to Himself."

"Ah, then you do know how to feel for me!"

"Yes, and let me tell you how I was comforted. I fear I was not quite submissive at first; but a dear, old mother in Christ, who had several times passed

259

through the same deep waters, came to me and said, 'My dear, the Lord gave you quite a little flock. And so, when He comes and asks you to return Him one, and you know He will keep it so safely in His kind arms and on His tender bosom, will you refuse? Can you not spare Him one?'

"Then my heart was almost broken to think I had been so churlish toward my beloved Master, and I resigned her cheerfully into His care. By and by, I grew happy in thinking of her, so safe from all sin and sorrow and pain and so full of joy at His right hand. I thought also of the time when my work shall be done, and I shall go to her."

Mrs. Chetwood thought for a moment, then turning to her friend with eyes brimful of tears, said, "Thank you. Your words have done me good. Surely I, too, can spare Him one. Had He taken all, what right could I have to complain? And oh, how sweet is the thought that He is caring so tenderly for my precious lambkin!"

The mothers mingled their tears again for a little — tears of blended grief and joy. Then Mrs. Chetwood said, "What else, dear friend? I seem to read in your eyes that you have something more to say to me."

"Only this, suggested to me by the same old Christian soldier and confirmed by my very own experience: that efforts to comfort others react upon ourselves, so proving the best panacea for our own sorrow. At least that is how it has been for me."

"I believe it. I am conscience-smitten that I have been so selfishly wrapped up in my own grief, and I shall set about the work at once. Will you do me the favor to suggest where I shall begin?"

Mrs. Keith spoke of Gotobed and the sort of comfort and assistance of which he stood in need.

Mrs. Chetwood shuddered. "Poor, poor fellow!" she said. "My heart aches for him. I feel sick at the very thought of seeing anyone in that mutilated condition, but I will go to him and do what I can for his comfort and relief."

"Thank you," returned Mrs. Keith heartily. "And please speak comfortingly to the poor mother. She is grieving very much for him, and she does not look well. One of the little girls, too, is quite ill with intermittent fever."

It was well that Mrs. Keith had engaged her friend to take up the labor of love, for it was long before she could resume it. On reaching home, she found Mildred sitting with Annis in her arms. The little one was moaning with pain and had a high fever.

"Mother, she is very sick," whispered Mildred tremulously, her eyes full of tears. She was thinking of how suddenly Mary Chetwood had been snatched away by the grim destroyer Death.

"I fear she is, poor darling! Poor little pet!" the mother said, bending over her and softly pressing her lips to the burning cheek.

"Oh, mother, mother, mother! If we should lose her . . ."

"We will do all we can to make her well, asking God's blessing on our efforts," Mrs. Keith answered with determined cheerfulness, though a sharp pang shot through her heart at the bare suggestion.

Dr. Grange was sent for at once. He pronounced the child very ill but by no means hopelessly so.

"The sickly season," he remarked, "is setting in unusually early and with uncommon severity, both in town and in the country. People are taken down with the fever every day, but it is what I have been expecting as the result of the long, heavy rains we had all through the spring succeeded by this intensely hot, dry weather. Why, we haven't had a drop of rain now, scarcely a cloud, for three weeks. The heavens above us are as brass, and the marshes and pools of stagnant water on every side are teeming with miasma.

"Keep the children and yourselves out of the sun during the heat of the day, and do not on any account allow them to be exposed to the night air and dew."

"Thank you for your suggestions," said Mr. Keith. "We will do our best to follow them."

He had just come home from his office, for it was near teatime. The children had come in from their work and play, and the whole family were gathered in the sitting room, where the baby lay in her cradle.

Fan had climbed on her father's knee and was lying quiet in his arms with her head on his shoulder.

The doctor, taking his hat to go, paused as his eye fell on her, and stepping quickly to her side, took her hand in his. "This child is sick, too," he said and went on to question and prescribe for her, directing that she should be put to bed at once.

"Oh," sighed Mildred, "if we only had Aunt Wealthy here!"

"I wish you had," the doctor said. "But all of the neighbors are always very kind in times of sickness."

"Yes, we have had experience of that in the past," replied Mrs. Keith.

The doctor called on Mrs. Chetwood and Mrs. Prior on his homeward way, and within an hour both were at Mr. Keith's offering their services in nursing or anything else that was needed.

"You are very kind," Mrs. Keith said, "but I think we can manage for a while. I think you should save your strength for those who need it more."

The little ones objected to being waited upon by strangers, and Celestia Ann insisted that she wanted no help with her housework or cooking, so the ladies departed after exacting a promise that they should be sent for if needed.

That time came soon. Before the crisis was passed with Annis and Fan, three more of the children— Zillah, Cyril, and Don—were taken down. Then father was stricken, and oh, what a weary burden of care, anxiety, toil, and grief fell upon the mother and sister! They had sore need now of all the faith, patience, and hope they had garnered up in happier days and of all the great and precious promises they had learned to lean upon.

Rupert was slowly dressing himself one August morning, feeling weak and ill, when his mother's pale, sorrowful face looked in his door.

He tried to brighten up and seem strong and well as he turned to meet her, asking, "How are you, mother dear? And the sick ones? I hope you all slept."

"Not much," she said, vainly striving after the accustomed cheery tone. "Annis and Fan did pretty well, and I am so thankful that the doctor considers them out of danger now, if we can only give them the good nursing they need. But poor Cyril is quite delirious. He is very, very sick, I fear, and Zillah is not much better. Besides—" but here her voice broke, and for a moment she was unable to go on.

"Oh, mother, not another one down?" he cried. "You and Mildred will be nigh unto killed with so much nursing."

"Rupert, it is your father now," she sobbed. "He tries to make us believe it is not much, that he'll sleep it off in an hour or so, but oh, I can see that he's very sick."

"My father very sick," he echoed, aghast. "Poor father! And you must lose his help with the others and have him to nurse, too!"

"That is not the worst of it. He is suffering and is perhaps in danger. Celestia Ann has breakfast nearly ready. I want you to eat at once, then go for the doctor—he did not come last night—and call and tell Mrs. Chetwood and Mrs. Prior what a sick household we are and that now if they can give me help in nursing, I shall be very glad and thankful."

Mrs. Keith moved on into the kitchen.

"Breakfast's on the table," said Celestia Ann. "You just sit down and eat, Mis' Keith, fer you look ready to drop. I'll pour you out a cup o' coffee, and then I'll run in and look after the sick till you're done."

"Thank you," Mrs. Keith said. "Though I have no desire for food, I will accept your offer, for I do feel faint and empty. Tell Mildred to come, too, as soon as she can be spared."

Rupert and Ada came in together at that moment and took their places at the table.

"Only three of us this morning, 'stead of ten," Ada remarked sadly.

"Well, we'll hope the others will all be back soon," said Rupert, longing to comfort and cheer his mother.

His head ached and chills crept down his back, but he said nothing about it, drank his coffee, forced himself to eat a little, and presently declaring himself done, put on his hat and hurried away on his errands.

It was now a fortnight since Annis had been taken ill, and not a drop of rain had fallen yet. The nights and mornings were chilly and damp, then the sun rose and shone all day with a fierce, burning heat that scorched everything it touched. And day by day, the fever had found its new victims till every physician's hands were full to overflowing.

"How chilly it is!" thought Rupert as he hastened down the path to the gate. "But it'll be hot enough presently," he said, looking up at the sky. "There is not a cloud to be seen, and the sun will be glaring down upon us as fiercely as ever. I think if there isn't some change in the climate soon, we'll all sicken and die."

He walked on up the street. Doors and windows were closed, and scarcely anyone seemed astir.

"They're all sleeping late," he thought. "Well, who can blame them? They're either sick themselves or worn out taking care of the sick."

He came first to the hotel. Mrs. Prior was very

busy getting breakfast, but she stepped to the door to hear his message.

"I'm dreadful sorry," she said. "I'll call round, tell your mother, just as soon as I can, but I've a half a dozen boarders down with the fever, and only one girl—the rest's all gone off to 'tend to their own folks, for the fever's bad all round in the country.

"I don't see how you can come at all then, Mrs. Prior," Rupert said. "I should think your hands must be more than full here at home."

"I'll come if I can, you may depend," she answered, "for I think a sight of your mother."

The boy sighed heavily as he turned and went on his way. How much of the brightness seemed to have gone out of life just then.

Dr. Grange's house was a few steps farther on. An old lady, the doctor's mother, answered his knock.

"The doctor is in bed and asleep just now," she said. "He has had very little rest for the last three weeks, was up all night out in the country, and came home with a heavy chill. The rest of the family are all down with the fever except myself and our little five-year-old Ellen.

"What are we coming to?" exclaimed the lad.

"I don't know," she answered, "but 'God is our refuge and strength; a very present help in trouble'!"

"I do not know what to do," said Rupert, looking sadly perplexed and anxious. "Mother says my father and Cyril are both very ill."

"I will tell the doctor when he awakens, and perhaps he will be able to go down. It would hardly be worthwhile to send you for another, for they're all equally busy."

"Thank you," he said, "we would not like to have to try another." Bidding her good morning, he went on his way to the squire's.

Mrs. Chetwood put on her bonnet at once and went with him.

"Claudina would come, too," she said, "but two of the boys are sick. I'm afraid she is taking the fever herself."

"It seems as if everybody is taking it," said Rupert. "Mrs. Chetwood, is it often so sickly here?"

"Never was known to be quite so bad before," she answered. "They say the oldest inhabitant doesn't remember such a time. Do you notice how quiet and empty the streets are?"

"Yes, ma'am. People seem to be very late in getting up. The stores are all shut up still."

"There's no business doing at all," she returned. "People are not up because they are ill—too ill, most of them, to even leave their beds.

"There are not many houses in town where more than one or two are able to crawl about to help themselves or wait on the sick. And Dr. Grange tells me it is just as bad in the country. The harvest is uncommonly fine, but there's nobody to gather it in.

"Emmaretta Lightcap died yesterday. I was there last night and helped to lay her out. All the rest of the family are in bed with the fever, except poor Gotobed and his mother.

"Oh, it's a sorrowful time! Effie and one or two of

the little ones are sick at Mr. Prescott's, and in the next house, not one of the family is able to be out of bed."

Mr. Keith was quite as ill as his wife feared.

She devoted herself principally to him, while Mrs. Chetwood and Mildred together nursed the others.

Rupert had had a chill, and a fever followed in due season. But he managed to keep up and conceal his illness from all but Celestia Ann, who did the best she could for him.

Mrs. Prior came in for an hour in the afternoon and, taking Mildred's place, enabled her to lie down for a little greatly needed rest and sleep.

Mrs. Chetwood spent the day and night with them but then went home to return no more. Her own family were no longer able to do without her care and nursing.

Zillah was slightly better that morning, but Mr. Keith, Cyril, and Don were all delirious and so evidently in danger that the hearts of mother and sister were very heavy.

Mrs. Keith scarcely left her husband's bedside except occasionally to pass into the next room and bend for a moment over her little boys, to take Annis or Fan in her arms to caress and reluctantly put them down again, and to whisper a word of hope and encouragement to Mildred, the other little girls, and Rupert.

Celestia Ann had full sway in the kitchen, and with genuine kindness of heart took charge of the rest of the house, so far as she could, and prepared delicacies for the sick.

She was a great help in looking after those who were convalescing. She had always a cheery word ready for the weary, anxious nurses, and in short proved herself invaluable in this great emergency.

What then was their distress and despair when they found they must lose her?

Glancing from the window on the morning of the second day after that which Mrs. Chetwood had spent with them, Mildred saw a countryman passing round toward the kitchen. In a moment, after his voice and Celestia Ann's could be heard in earnest colloquy, the latter interrupted with heavy sobs.

Then she appeared at the door of the nursery with her apron to her eyes and silently beckoned to Mildred to come to her.

"What is it?" the latter asked, going to her.

"Why, my brother's come to fetch me home, and I'll have to go, bad as I hate to leave you. I should-n't, for I don't see how you're agoin' to git along without me."

"Nor I," said Mildred, aghast. "Oh, Celestia Ann, must you go?"

"Yes, can't help it. They're all down with the fever, 'cept mother—and she's poorly—and this brother that's come after me. He's got a chill on him now, he says. So I'll have to pick up my duds and be off right away."

"Yes, of course you must go to your own when they need you," said Mildred, "unless they could get someone else. Oh, Celestia Ann, don't you think it possible they could?"

"No, I know they can't, Miss Mildred. There's no help to be get these days for love or money; and the Lord only knows what's to become of us all!

"Sam says there's several died in our neighborhood a'ready, just for want o' good nussin' and proper victuals, so the doctor says."

"And just so it will be with us," sobbed Mildred, sinking into a chair and covering her face with her hands. "I cannot nurse them all properly and cook what they need to eat. Oh, it is so terrible to think they must die for want of it."

"It's awful, and I'm dreadful sorry for you and everybody," sighed Celestia Ann, wiping away the tears that were streaming over her cheeks. "Maybe you might git Mis' Rood to come in for a few days. I'll git Sam to go and see while I'm a pickin' up my things.

"She ain't much for cookin', I don't suppose, but she could clean up, do that big washin', and help a liftin' the sick ones. That is, if she'll come. I dunno, but she may be down sick herself."

Sam kindly undertook the errand, but alas, Mrs. Rood was down sick herself, and no help could be had from that quarter nor apparently from any other. With many tears and sobs Celestia Ann took her departure, saying, "I'll come back as soon as I kin, if I keep well and my folks gits able to do without me."

# CHAPTER
# TWENTY-FOURTH

*Calamity is man's true touchstone.*

IT WAS TO Mildred that Celestia Ann's parting words were spoken, Mildred sitting in dumb despair beside the bed where Cyril and Don lay tossing and moaning in a burning fever. Her heart sank like lead in her bosom as she listened to the rumbling of the wheels of the wagon that was bearing away her late efficient helper. "What could they do without her?"

A quiet step crossed the room, and a soft hand was laid caressingly on Mildred's bowed head. Looking up, she saw her mother's sweet, pale face bending over her. It was a well-worn and weary face but had a strange peacefulness shining through its care and sorrow.

"Oh, mother, mother, whatever shall we do?" cried the girl in a broken whisper and with a burst of tears.

Mrs. Keith had a small Bible in her hand, her finger between the leaves. She laid it open before Mildred, pointed to a passage in the Sixty-second

Psalm, and just touching her lips to her daughter's forehead, turned to the little sufferers on the bed.

"Mother's darlings! Mother's poor little men! Try to be very patient and good like the dear Lord Jesus when he was in pain, and mother hopes you will soon be well again. She is asking Jesus to make you well."

"I wish He would," moaned Cyril, while Don uttered some incoherent words, showing that his mind wandered.

"I'se better, mamma," piped the baby voice of Annis from another bed. "Fan and me's better. I dess Dod will make us well, 'tause we asked Him to."

"Yes, mother. Don't fret about us," joined in Fan and Zillah patiently.

She went over and kissed all three, calling them "dear good children," then went into the kitchen.

Rupert was there trying to make a custard. Ada was washing dishes.

"You see, you're not entirely without help in this department yet, mother," the lad said laughingly.

"No," she answered with a smile that he felt was ample reward for his efforts. "How are you succeeding?"

"Barely. At least it looks nice. Please come and tell me if 'tis ready to be taken off."

"It will be in a moment. Run out and get me a handful of leaves from that young peach tree to flavor it with."

He obeyed, she stirring the custard and brightly commending Ada's industry while he was gone.

"Here they are, mother. Is this enough?" he asked, coming back.

"Quite," she said, taking them from him. Then, as her hand touched his, "Rupert," she cried in anguish, "you are sick—burning up with fever!"

"Just heated over the stove, mother," he said, trying to laugh it off as he lifted the kettle from the fire and poured its contents into a bowl.

"No, I am not to be deceived," she answered in a choking voice. "You ought to be in bed now."

He shook his head. "Somebody must keep up—several somebodies—to take anything like proper care of the sick ones. And, mother, I'm as able as you are. You look dreadfully worn and ill."

She was all that. She felt the chills creeping over her at that moment, and her head seemed ready to burst, her heart also.

Oh, she had need of all the comfort and support of the words she had pointed out to Mildred and of the exhortation contained therein.

"'My soul, wait thou only upon God; for my expectation is from Him. He only is my rock and my salvation; He is my defense, I shall not be moved. In God is my salvation and my glory; the rock of my strength and my refuge is in God.'"

She whispered them to herself as with clasped hands and closed eyes she sank heavily into a chair, half-unconscious of what she was doing.

Rupert sprang to her side, thinking she was about to faint, and Ada, with the same thought, set down the plate she was wiping and hurried to her also.

They caught the last words: "The rock of my strength and my refuge is in God."

"Yes, mother dear," sobbed the lad, putting his arms around her. "Oh, you know it's a refuge that will never fail. 'Therefore will we not fear, though the earth be removed and though the mountains be carried into the midst of the sea.' 'Man's extremity is God's opportunity,' and He will help us through this strait somehow."

"Yes," she whispered, "and though it should be by death, what is that but going home? To those of us who love the Lord and trust in His imputed righteousness," she added, looking earnestly and questioningly into his face.

"Mother, I believe I do," he said, "though I have never told you so before."

"Now I can bear it," she whispered, closing her eyes again while a sweet smile played about her lips.

Her head dropped heavily on her son's shoulder.

"Oh," shrieked Ada, "she's dying! Mother's dying!"

"Hush!" cried Rupert sternly, thinking of the mischief her cry might work should it reach the ears of the sick ones. "She has only fainted. A tumbler of water. Quick, quick, Ada!"

As the terrified child hastened to do his bidding, Mildred came flying from the inner room, her face pale, her whole frame trembling with fright.

"Mother!" the word came in tones of agony from her pale, quivering lips.

"It's only a faint," said Rupert hoarsely. "Help me to lay her down and loosen her clothes. And haven't you hartshorn or something like it to bring her around?"

"Yes. Ada, quick, quick! The bottle of smelling salts! It's on the stand by father's bedside. Oh, mother, mother! You, too! What's to become of us? Oh, Rupert, she's just killed with nursing! And I couldn't help it."

"Of course, you couldn't. You are nearly killed yourself," he said, his tears falling almost as fast as hers, while between them they half-carried, half-dragged the insensible form into the adjoining room and laid her tenderly down upon a lounge.

Poor children! So utterly overwhelmed were they by their mother's helpless condition—in addition to all the other causes for anxiety, perplexity, and distress—and so taken up with efforts for her restoration to consciousness that they scarcely heard the cries of the sick little ones, who could not understand why they were thus left alone, or the calls of their father, who had roused from sleep and missed his gentle nurse. Nor did they notice who it was that came in through the open kitchen door and silently assisted them, raising the window blind and sprinkling water on the still, white face.

At last, Mrs. Keith's eyes opened, and she started up, asking faintly, "What is it? Have I been ill?" Then she fell back again, completely exhausted.

"You were faint, mother dear," said Mildred, vainly striving to steady her voice. "But you just lie still for a while, and I hope you will get over it. You have been doing far too much, and you must rest now."

"Rest, child! How can I? There is your father calling me, and the children are crying!"

She started up again but with the same result as before.

"My poor, sick husband! My little, ailing children! What is to become of you?" she sighed, tears stealing from beneath the closed eyelids and trickling down the pale cheeks.

"Mother, I will do my best," sobbed Mildred. "Only lie and rest yourself."

"And I am here to assist and able to do it," said a somewhat harsh, discordant voice, though there was in it a tone of kindness, too.

Then they looked up and saw, standing near, the stiff, angular figure of Damaris Drybread.

"You?" Mildred exclaimed in utter surprise.

"Yes, I, Miss Keith. Did you think there was none of the milk of human kindness in me? My school's broken up by this pestilence, and only one of our family has took the fever yet. So, when I heard that you were nearly all down sick here and your girl had gone off and left you, I said to myself, 'There's a duty for you there, Damaris Drybread. Go right away and do it.' And I came."

"And it was very, very kind of you," Mildred said, extending her hand. "I have hardly deserved it from you, for I've judged you harshly."

"Well, I shouldn't wonder if I'd done the same to you," Damaris answered coldly, taking the offered hand only to drop it again instantly. "But that's neither here nor there, and I don't ask no thanks. I'm only tryin' to be a good Samaritan to you, because we're told, 'Go and do thou likewise.'"

The cries of the children had become so piteous and importunate that Mildred rushed away to attend to them.

Her father's calls had ceased, and as the little ones quieted down, she could hear a manly voice speaking to him in gentle, soothing tones.

"It is the doctor," she thought with an emotion somewhat akin to pleasure. He was so sorely needed and had not called since the previous night, but on going in, she found Mr. Lord by the bedside.

He turned, showing a face full of sympathy and concern, and held out his hand.

"This is kind," she said, putting hers into it.

"My poor child!" he responded feelingly, raising the hand to his lips in his absent way. "My heart aches for you, and there are many others in like affliction—many others! All round the country people are sick and dying, many of them simply for lack of suitable nourishment."

The tears rolled down his manly cheeks as he spoke, and the sight of them did not lower him in the girl's esteem.

"And what can I do?" he went on. "I know nothing of cooking; I can only carry them crackers to sustain their poor bodies and try to feed their souls with the bread of life. I feel for them all, but for you—oh, Mildred, dear girl, what can I do to help and comfort you in this extremity?"

"We have need of nurses. Mother—"

But with that word, she broke into uncontrollable weeping, suppressed, for fear of disturbing her father, who had fallen into a doze, but shaking her whole frame with its violence.

It distressed her listener. He took a step toward her, a gesture, as if he would fold her in his arms. But he drew hastily back, blushing and confused, as the door opened, and Dr. Grange came in.

# CHAPTER
# TWENTY-FIFTH

*All love is sweet,*
*Given or returned. Common as light is love,*
*And its familiar voice wearies not ever.*

—SHELLEY

"AH, GOOD MORNING, my dear child! Good morning, sir," the doctor said in an undertone, giving his hand to Mildred and the minister in turn. Then with an anxious glance at the bed, he said, "How is he? Sleeping now, I see. How did he rest through the night?"

"Not very well, and—"

"Your mother? Where is she? Not down, too?" he said with almost a groan as he read the truth in the young girl's face.

Mildred led him to her. She lay on the lounge still, with closed eyes and a face of deathly pallor, her cheek resting against the dark curls of Rupert, who had thrown himself on the floor by her side and laid his head on the same pillow while he held one of her hands, caressing it tenderly.

His cheeks were burning, his eyes sparkling with fever.

The doctor glanced from one to the other. "Ought to be in bed, both of you. Go, my boy, at once. You are not fit to be here."

"I can't, sir. I'm needed to take care of the others."

"You will help most by giving up at once," said the doctor. "Otherwise, you will make yourself so sick as to need a great deal of attention."

"Yes, go, my dear boy," whispered Mrs. Keith.

"I will, since you bid me, darling mother," he answered, pressing his hot lips to her cheek, then tottering from the room.

She looked after him with sad, pitying eyes, "So sick, and your mother not able to nurse you! Mildred, my poor dear child, how are you to stand it?" she sighed, turning them upon her daughter's face, as she bent over her.

"Try not to be troubled and anxious, my dear madam," said the doctor. "The more quiet and free from care you can keep your mind, the better for you. Trust the Lord that all will come out right."

"I will. He is all my hope and trust, for myself and for my dear ones," she answered with almost her accustomed cheerfulness. "Things look very dark, but 'behold the Lord's hand is not shortened that it cannot save; neither his ear heavy that it cannot hear.'"

"And He has sent us some help already," observed Mildred, "from a most unexpected quarter."

Damaris came in at that moment from the kitchen, saluted the doctor in her usual formal way, and turning to Mrs. Keith, remarked, "I hope you're not going to be very sick, but you'd ought to go to bed for today, anyhow. Don't you say so, doctor?"

"I do most emphatically," answered the physician, who had seated himself at the table and was busy measuring out medicines. "And I'm very glad, Miss Damaris, to see you here."

"It appeared to me my duty to come," she said, looking not ill-pleased. "I'm no great nurse, but I can do housework and cook for sick or well, and them things is as necessary as the nursing."

"Certainly," said Dr. Grange, and the physician went on to give directions to her concerning the proper food for his patients, and to Mildred in regard to the administering of medicines and other remedies.

He made his round, pronounced Zillah much better, and Mr. Keith slightly so. He was silent as to the little boys, and Mildred's heart was full of anguish as she perceived from his countenance, or thought she did, that their recovery was still very doubtful.

Mr. Lord had remained at Mr. Keith's bedside while the doctor and Mildred were absent from the room, and he was still there when they returned. He looked perplexed and ill at ease.

"I have no skill in nursing," he said, "never have had any experience. I am in fact a very unsuitable person for the task, being absent-minded, as you both know. But if I can be of any service, I—Miss Mildred, I can sit here and hand anything he asks for, call you if he needs your assistance, and give the medicines, if you will be good enough to remind me when it is time to do so."

The offer was gladly accepted, and the new nurse entered upon his duties immediately.

Yet even with these new and unexpected helps, it was clearly impossible for the weary girl to give proper attention to five very sick persons and two who were barely convalescent. Her heart was overwhelmed, the burden heavier than she could possibly bear.

But blessed be God. His people need not bear griefs and anxieties alone; He bids them not.

"Cast thy burden upon the Lord, and He shall sustain thee." "Call upon Me in the day of trouble. I will deliver thee, and thou shalt glorify me."

These and others like great and precious promises were brought home with power and sweetness to Mildred's mind in this time of deep distress and anguish, and kept her from sinking beneath the load.

"Oh, Lord of hosts, blessed is the man that trusteth in thee." "For thou, Lord, wilt bless the righteous; with favor wilt thou compass him as with a shield."

There seemed no earthly friend left to come to Mildred's aid. She could think of none. Claudina Chetwood and Lucilla Grange were both themselves lying upon sick beds. So were her lady acquaintances in Pleasant Plains except such as, like herself, had their hands more than full with the care of the sick in their own families. Aunt Wealthy was so far, far away that, before a message could reach her, they might all be in their graves.

How long it seemed since she went away! How long since the beginning of this dreadful sickly season that had, as it were, shut Mildred away from all pleasant social interaction with her young companions into her own little world of trial and trouble!

It was a comfort that someone was attending to domestic affairs and someone was sitting with her sick father and Rupert, who now shared his bed. But, ah, she could not more than half-attend to the pressing needs of the others.

The day was intensely hot, scarcely a breath of air stirring, though every door and window stood wide open. The little boys were feverish and restless and wanted to be fanned every moment. They called almost incessantly for cold, fresh water.

The others craved it, too, and it could be had only from the spring at the foot of the steep riverbank. Ice being an unknown luxury in Pleasant Plains at that period, it could not be kept cool for any length of time.

She did not feel at liberty to call upon either Miss Drybread or Mr. Lord for this service, and as the one judged it unnecessary that the water should be brought frequently and the other was too absentminded to think of offering to bring it—and she could not leave her charges to go herself, even if her strength had been equal to the effort in addition to all the other demands upon it—she could but endure the pain of seeing the loved ones suffer from thirst.

"Water, water. Cold water, Milly," sobbed little Don.

"This is cold water, dear," she said, holding a cup to his lips.

"No, 'tisn't right cold," he fretted, pushing it away. "It doesn't taste good. Oh, send somebody to bring cold, *cold* water!"

She set down the cup and burst into tears.

Absorbed in her grief and distress, she did not hear the gate gently opened and shut again or a step coming up the path, across the porch, through the hall, and into the room where she sat weeping such bitter tears as she had never wept before.

But it was a cautious tread, as of one who feared to disturb the sick, as was the fact. With that fear before his eyes, Wallace Ormsby had thought even to come in slippered feet.

He should have paused at the room door till invited to enter, but he forgot everything else at the sight of Mildred's distress and never stopped till he was close at her side.

"Oh, Mildred, dear Mildred, what is it? What can I do to help and comfort you?" he said in tones tremulous with love and pity as he bent over her and took her hand in his.

She started with surprise, but the hand was not withdrawn. The lips and eyes smiled faintly through the rain of tears, as she looked up into his noble face and read there ardent affection and deep sympathy for her sorrow.

"Surely you will let me help you in this dreadful time when there's no more proper person to do it?" he said with earnest entreaty. "Why should we care for conventionalities now? You are weak and worn out and in sore need of assistance. I am well and strong, able, and more than willing to give it. Say, may I not stay here by your side and help with this nursing?"

"Water, cold water!" sobbed Don. "Oh, go get cold water for me and Cyril."

"Yes, Wallace, Mr. Ormsby," Mildred said, the tears coursing down her cheeks. "I cannot sacrifice them to conventionalities, so I gladly accept your kind offer of help."

"Oh, don't talk! Go get water, quick!" fretted Don. "I can't wait. Milly, what makes you so naughty to me?"

Wallace seized a pitcher standing near and hastened to the spring. He was no stranger to the premises and knew the way.

For the next fortnight, he had what he considered the blessed privilege of sharing Mildred's burdens, griefs, and cares, watching with her over each of those dear ones as they passed through the crisis of the disease and the first stages of convalescence. They all recovered, a fact which the parents and older children recognized with deep heart-felt gratitude to Him to whom "belong the issues from death."

Nor did they forget the thanks due their earthly helpers and friends. The minister held a warmer place than before in the hearts of these parishioners, and Damaris Drybread received a substantial reward for her services, which, as she was dependent upon her own exertions for a livelihood, was not declined.

That fearful sickly season finally passed away, but it was not soon to be forgotten by the survivors. Comparative health and prosperity again dawned upon the town and surrounding country.

The Keiths returned to their old busy, cheerful life, and Wallace Ormsby, beloved by the whole family, seemed as one of them. Years of ordinary social interaction could not have brought him into so close an intimacy with them, especially Mildred, as those two weeks in which the two shared the toils, the cares, and the anxieties of those who watch by beds of sickness that may end in death.

They had learned to know each other's faults and weaknesses, strong points and virtues, and with that knowledge, their mutual esteem and admiration had increased. They had been warm friends before, but now they were—not plighted lovers, for Ormsby had not spoken yet—but . . .

*To his eye*
*There was but one beloved face on earth,*
*And that was shining on him.*

## THE END

# *The Original Elsie Classics*

Elsie Dinsmore
Elsie's Holidays at Roselands
Elsie's Girlhood
Elsie's Womanhood
Elsie's Motherhood
Elsie's Children
Elsie's Widowhood
Grandmother Elsie
Elsie's New Relations
Elsie at Nantucket
The Two Elsies
Elsie's Kith and Kin
Elsie's Friends at Woodburn
Christmas with Grandma Elsie
Elsie and the Raymonds
Elsie Yachting with the Raymonds
Elsie's Vacation
Elsie at Viamede
Elsie at Ion
Elsie at the World's Fair
Elsie's Journey on Inland Waters
Elsie at Home
Elsie on the Hudson
Elsie in the South
Elsie's Young Folks
Elsie's Winter Trip
Elsie and Her Loved Ones
Elsie and Her Namesakes